The Heart of a Dog

Albert Payson Terhune

The Heart of a Dog

ISBN: 978-1-64799-870-7

MY BOOK IS DEDICATED TO

MY FRIEND
MARK SAXTON
THE ONLY BOY WHOM THE CONSERVATIVE
SUNNYBANK COLLIES HAVE HONOURED WITH THEIR
FRIENDSHIP, AND WHOM THEY HAVE ACCEPTED
AS A LOVED PLAYFELLOW

CONTENTS

ONE

Fox!

When the Stippled Silver Kennel, Inc., went into the wholesale raising of silver foxes for a world market, its two partners brought to the enterprise a comfortable working capital and an uncomfortable ignorance of the brain-reactions of a fox.

They had visited the National Exhibition of silver foxes. They had spent days at successful fox farms, studying every detail of management and memorising the rigid diet-charts. They had committed to memory every fact and hint in Bulletin No. 1151 of the United States Department of Agriculture—issued for the help of novice breeders of silver foxes.

They had mastered each and every available scrap of exact information concerning the physical welfare of captive silver foxes. But, for lack of half a lifetime's close application to the theme, their knowledge of fox mentality and fox nature was nil.

Now one may raise chickens or hogs or even cattle, without taking greatly into account the inner workings of such animals' brains. But no man yet has made a success of raising foxes or their fifth cousin, the collie, without spending more time in studying out the mental than the physical beast.

On the kitchen wall of the Stippled Silver Kennel, Inc., was the printed dietary of silver foxes. On the one library shelf of the kennel was all the available literature on silver fox breeding, from government pamphlets to a three-volume monograph. In the four-acre space within the kennel enclosure were thirty model runways, twenty by twenty feet; each equipped with a model shelter-house and ten of them further fitted out with model brood nests.

In twenty-four of these thirty model runways abode twenty-four model silver foxes, one to each yard at this autumn season—twenty-four silver foxes, pedigreed and registered—foxes whose lump value was something more than $7,400. Thanks to the balanced rations and meticulous care lavished on them, all twenty-four were in the pink of form.

All twenty-four seemed as nearly contented as can a wild thing which no longer has the zest of gambling with death for its daily food and which is stared at with indecent closeness and frequency by dread humans.

1

But the partners of the Stippled Silver Kennel, Inc., failed to take note, among other things, of the uncanny genius certain foxes possess for sapping and mining; nor that some foxes are almost as deft at climbing as is a cinnamon bear. True, the average silver fox is neither a gifted burrower nor climber. But neither are such talents rare.

For example, King Whitefoot II, in Number 8 run, could have given a mole useful hints in underground burrowing. Lady Pitchdark, the temperamental young vixen in Number 17 run, might wellnigh have qualified as the vulpine fly. Because neither of these costly specimens spent their time in sporadic demonstration of their arts, in the view of humans, those same humans did not suspect the accomplishments.

Then came an ice-bright moonlit night in late November—a night to stir every quadruped's blood to tingling life and to set humans to crouching over fireplaces. Ten minutes after Rance and Ethan Venner, the kennel partners, finished their perfunctory evening rounds of the yards, King Whitefoot II was blithely at work.

Foxes and other burrowing beasts seek instinctively the corners or the edges of yards, when striving to dig a way out. Any student of their ways will tell you that. Wherefore, as in most fox-kennels, the corners and inner edges of the Stippled Silver yards were fringed with a half-yard of mesh-wire, laid flat on the ground.

Whitefoot chose a spot six inches on the hither edge of a border-wire and began his tunnel. He did not waste strength by digging deep. He channelled a shallow tube, directly under the flat-laid wire. Indeed, the wire itself formed the top of his tunnel. The frost was not yet deep enough or hard enough to impede his work. Nor, luckily for him, did he have to circumnavigate any big underground rock.

In forty-two minutes from the time he began to dig, his pointed black nose and his wide-cheeked stippled black face was emerging into the open, a few inches outside his yard.

Wriggling out of his tunnel, he shook himself daintily to rid his shimmering silver-flecked black coat of such dirt as clung to it. Then he glanced about him. From the nearby wire runs, twenty-three pairs of slitted topaz eyes flamed avidly at him. Twenty-three ebony bodies crouched moveless; the moon glinting bright on their silver stipples and snowy tailtips.

The eyes of his world were on the fugitive. The nerves of his world were taut and vibrant with thrill at his escapade. But they were sportsmen in their own way, these twenty-three prisoners who looked on while their more skilled fellow won his way to liberty. Not

2

a whine, not so much as a deep-drawn breath gave token of the excitement that was theirs. No yelping bark brought the partners out to investigate. These captives could help their comrade only by silence. And they gave him silence to a suffocating degree.

With their round phosphorous eyes they followed his every move. But twenty-two of the twenty-three forbore so much as a single motion whose sound might attract human ears. Couchant, aquiver, turning their heads ever so little and in unison to watch his progress, the twenty-two watched Whitefoot make for the high wire boundary fence which encircled the four-acre kennel enclosure—the fence beyond whose southern meshes lay the frost-spangled meadow.

Beyond the meadow reared the naked black woods, sloping stiffly upward to the mountain whose sides they draped;—the mountain which was the outpost of the wilderness hinterland to southward of this farm-valley.

But, as Whitefoot set to work at the absurdly simple exploit of digging under this outer fence—a fence not extending underground and with no flat width of wire before it—the twenty-third prisoner could stand the emotional strain no longer. Young and with nerves less steady than her companions', little Lady Pitchdark marred the perfect symphony of noiselessness.

She did not bark or even yelp. But she went into action.

By natural genius she was a climber. Up the side of her ten-foot run-wire she whizzed; her long-clawed feet scarce seeming to seek toe-hold in the ladder of meshes they touched. Like a cat, she sped upward.

To provide against such an unlikely effort at jail-breaking, the four wire walls of the run sloped slightly inward. At their summit, all around, was a flat breadth of wire that hung out for eight inches over the run; projecting inside the walls. As a rule such deterrents were quite enough to bar an ordinary fox from escape. But nature had taught Lady Pitchdark more than she teaches the ordinary fox. She was one of the rare vulpines born with climbing-genius.

Up she scrambled her fierce momentum carrying her to the very top of the fence; to the spot where it merged with the eight-inch overhang. Here, by every rule, the vixen should have yielded to the immutable law of gravity and should have tumbled back to the ground with a breath-expelling flop.

This is precisely what she did not do. Still helped by her momentum, she clawed frantically with both forefeet at the edge of the overhang. Her claws hooked in its end-meshes. Her hindfeet released their hold on the in-slanting fence and she swung for an

3

instant between moon and earth—a glowing black swirl of fur, shot with a myriad silver threads.

Then lithely she drew herself up, on the overhang. A pause for breath and she was skidding down the steep slope of the fence's outer side. A dart across the yard and she reached the kennel's boundary fence just as Whitefoot was squirming to freedom through the second and shorter tunnel he had made that night.

Diving through, so close behind him that her outthrust muzzle brushed his sensitive tailtip, Pitchdark reached the safety of the outer world at almost the same instant as did he. Whitefoot felt the light touch at his tail. He spun around, snarling murderously, his razor-keen teeth bared. He had won his way to liberty by no slight exercise of brain and of muscle. He was not minded to surrender tamely to any possible pursuer.

But as he confronted the slender young vixen in her royal splendour of pelt and with her unafraid excited eyes fixed so mischievously upon him, the dog-fox's lips slipped down from their snarling curl; sheathing the fearsome array of teeth and tushes. For a fraction of a second Whitefoot and Pitchdark faced each other there under the dazzling white moon; twin ebon blotches on the frost-strewn grass. Twenty-two pairs of yellow-fire eyes were upon them.

Then on impulse the two refugees touched noses. As though by this act they established common understanding, they wheeled about as one; and galloped silently, shoulder to shoulder, across the frosted meadow to the safety of the black mountainside forest.

Sportsmanship can go only just so far; even in cool-nerved foxes. As the couple vanished through the night, a shrilly hideous multiple clamour of barking went up from twenty-two furry black throats. The tense hush was broken by a bedlam of raucous noise. The prisoners dashed themselves against the springy sides of their wire runs. One and another of them made desperate scrambling attempts to climb the inslanting walls that encircled them—only to fall back to the frozen ground and add their quota once more to the universal din.

Rance and Ethan Venner came tumbling out of the nearby house, grasping their flashlights and shouting confusedly to each other. Instantly blank silence overspread the yards. The foxes crouched low, eyes aflame, staring mutely at the belated humans.

The briefest of inspections told the brothers what had happened. First they found the tunnel leading forth from Whitefoot's run. Then they discovered that Pitchdark's run was empty; though they could find no clue to its occupant's mysterious

4

vanishing until next morning's sunrise showed them a tuft of finespun black fur stuck to a point of wire on the overhang, ten feet above ground. Last of all the partners came upon the hole under the fence which divided the kennel from the meadow.

"Whitefoot was worth an easy $600 as he stood," grunted Rance Venner, miserably; as his flashlight's ray explored the hole under the fence. "Nearer $700, in the coat he's carrying this fall. And Pitchdark isn't more'n a couple of hundred dollars behind him. Two of the best we had. A hundred per cent loss; just as we're getting started."

"Nope," contradicted Ethan. "Not a hundred per cent loss. Only about fifty. The pelt of either one of 'em will bring $300, dressed. Any of a dozen dealers will pay us that for it."

"If they was to pay us three million, we wouldn't be any richer," complained Rance. "We haven't got the pelts to sell. You're talking plumb foolish, Ethan."

"We'll have 'em both by noon to-morrow," declared Ethan. "Those two foxes were born in a kennel. They don't know anything else. They're as tame as pet squirrels. We'll start out gunning for 'em at sunrise. We'll take Ruby along. She'll scent 'em, double quick. Then all we'll have to do is plant the shots where they won't muss the pelt too much."

"We'll do better'n that," supplemented Rance, his spirits rising at his brother's tone of confidence. "We won't shoot 'em. We'll get out the traps, instead. They're both tame and neither of 'em ever had to hustle for a meal. They'll walk right into the traps, as quick as they get the sniff of cooked food. C'mon in and help me put the traps in shape. We ought to be setting 'em before sunrise. The two foxes will be scouting for breakfast by that time."

The newly optimistic Rance was mistaken in all his forecasts. The two fugitives were not scouting for breakfast at sunrise. Hours earlier they twisted their way in through the narrow little opening of an unguarded chicken-house belonging to a farm six miles from the kennel. Thither they were drawn by the delicious odour of living prey.

There, like a million foxes since the birth of time, they slew without noise or turmoil. There they glutted themselves; carrying away each a heavy fowl for future feasting; bearing off their plunder in true vulpine fashion with the weight of the bird slung scientifically over the bearer's withers.

Daybreak found them lying snugly asleep in a hollow windfall tree that was open at either end and which lay lengthwise of a nick in the hillside, with briars forming an effective hedge all about it.

5

Nor did the best casting efforts of Ruby, the partners' foxhound, succeed in following their cleverly confused trail across a pool and two brooks. In the latter brook, they had waded for nearly a furlong before emerging on dry ground at the same side.

Thus set in a winter of bare sustenance for the runaways. They kept to no settled abiding place, but drifted across country; feasting at such few farmsteads as had penetrable hencoops; doing wondrous teamwork in the catching of rabbits and partridges; holing in under windfalls or in rock-clefts when blizzards made the going bad.

It was the season when foxes as a rule run solitary. Seldom in early winter do they hunt in pairs and never at any season in packs. But these two black and silver waifs were bound together not only by early association but by mutual inexperience of the wild. And while this inexperience did not blur nor flaw their marvellous instinct, they found it more profitable to hunt together than alone.

Only once or twice in their winter's foraging did they chance upon any of the high-country's native red foxes. A heavy hunting season had shifted most of the reds to a distant part of the county; as is the way with foxes that are overpressed by the attentions of trappers and hounds. In that region, pink coats and hunting horses and foxhound packs were unknown. But many a mountain farmer eked out his lean income by faring afield with a brace of disreputable but reliable mongrel hounds and a fowling piece as disreputably reliable; eager for the flat price of $10 to $12 per skin offered by the nearest wholesale dealer. This sum of course was for the common red fox; silver foxes being as unknown to the region at large as were dinosaurs.

(The dealer paid the farmer-huntsman perhaps $11 per skin. The pelt was then cured and dressed and mounted and equipped with snappers; at a total price in labour and material of perhaps $6 at most. After which, in marketable form, it sold at retail from $60 to $75 or even higher. Thus, there was money for every one concerned—except possibly for the ultimate buyer.)

The two silver foxes had the forest and farmland largely to themselves. The few reds they met did not attack them or affiliate with them at that hungry time of year.

The winter winds and the ice-storms made Whitefoot's coat shine and thicken as never had it done on scientifically balanced rations. The life of the wild put new depth to Pitchdark's narrow chest and gave her muscular power and sinew to spare. Quizzical Dame Nature had lifted them from man's wisest care; as though in object lesson of her own infinitely more efficient methods for conditioning her children.

6

Late January brought a sore-throat thaw and with it a melting of drift and ice-pack. Incidentally it ushered in the yearly vulpine mating season.

Spring was early that year. But before the frost was out of the ground, Pitchdark had chosen her nursery. It was by no means so elaborate nor sanitary as had been the costly brood-nests at the kennel. Indeed it would have struck horror to the heart of any scientific breeder.

For it was merely a woodchuck hole in an upland meadow, at the forest edge, a short mile from a straggling farmstead. Even here Whitefoot's inspired prowess as a digger was not called into play. His sole share toward securing the home was to thrash the asthmatically indignant old woodchuck that had dug the burrow. Then Pitchdark made her way cautiously down the hole and proceeded to enlarge it a little at the shallow bottom. That was all the home-making done by the pair.

Then, of a windy night, just before the first of April, the vixen did not join her mate in his expedition for loot. And as he panted homeward before dawn with a broken-winged quail between his jaws, he found her lying in the burrow's hollow, with five indeterminate-looking babies nuzzling close to her soft side.

Then began days, or rather nights, of double foraging for Whitefoot. For it is no light thing to provide food for a den-ridden mate and, indirectly, for five hungry and husky cubs.

Nor was the season propitious for food-finding. The migratory birds, for the most part, had not shifted north. The rabbits for some silly reason of their own had changed their feeding grounds to the opposite valley. Farmers had suffered too many depredations from Whitefoot and Pitchdark during the past month to leave their henroosts as hospitably open as of yore.

The first day's hunting netted only a sick crow that had tumbled from a tree. Whitefoot turned with disgust from this find. For, though he would have been delighted to dine on the rankest of carrion, yet in common with all foxes, he could not be induced to touch any bird of prey.

That night he foraged again; in spite of having outraged his regular custom by hunting in daylight. There was no fun in hunting, this night. For a wild torrent of rain had burst out of the black clouds which all day had been butting their way across the windy sky.

Foxes detest rain, and this rain was a veritable deluge; a flood that started the spring freshets and turned miles of bottomland into soggy lakes. Yet Whitefoot kept on. Grey dawn found him midway between his lair and the farmstead at the foot of the hill.

This farm he and Pitchdark had avoided. It was too near their den for safe plundering. Its human occupants might well be expected to seek the despoilers. And just then those despoilers were in no condition to elude the chase. Wherefore, fox-fashion, the two had ranged far afield and had reserved the nearby farm for later emergencies.

Now the emergency appeared to call for such a visit from Whitefoot. A moment or so he hesitated, irresolute whether to return empty-mouthed to his mate or to go first to the farm for possible food. He decided on the farm.

Had he gone to the burrow he would have known there was no further need to forage for those five beautiful baby silvers, so different in aspect from the slaty-gray infants of the red fox. A swelling rivulet of rain had been deflected from its downhill course by a wrinkle in the soil; and had poured swishingly down the opening of the woodchuck warren and thence down into the ill-constructed brood nest at its bottom.

For the safeguarding of newborn fox-babies, as of the babies of every race, dry warmth is all-essential. Chilled and soaked, despite their young mother's frantic efforts to protect them, the five ill-nourished and perilously inbred cubs ceased to nurse and began to squeak right dolefully. Then, one by one they died. The last of them stiffened out, just before daybreak.

Rance and Ethan Venner would have cursed luridly at loss of so many hundred dollars in potential peltry. But the bereft little mother only cuddled her ice-cold babies the closer; crooning piteously to them. They were her first litter. She could not realise what had befallen them, nor why one and all of them had ceased to nurse.

Meantime, her mate was drifting like an unobtrusive black shadow through the rain toward the clutter of farm buildings at the base of the hill-pasture. His scent told him there was a dog somewhere in that welter of sheds and barns and houses. But his scent told him also that there were fowls aplenty. Preparing to match his speed and his wit against any dog's, he crept close and closer, taking due advantage of every patch of cover; unchecked even by the somewhat more distant man-scent; and urged on by that ever stronger odour of live chickens.

Presently he was skirting the chicken-yard. It and its coop were too fast-locked for him to hope to enter with less than a half-hour's clever digging. He had not a half-hour. He had not a half-minute to spare.

Slinking from the coop, he rounded a tool-house. There he

8

halted. For to his nostrils came again the smell of living food, though of a sort vaguely unpleasant to him. Hunger and the need to feed his brood formed too strong a combination for this faint distaste to combat.

He peered around the corner of the half-open door of the tool-house. From the interior arose the hated dog-smell, ten times stronger than before. But he knew by nose and by hearing that the dog was no longer in there.

He was correct in this, as in most of his surmises. Not five minutes earlier, the early-rising Dick Logan had opened the tool-house door and convoyed thence his pedigreed collie, Jean, to the kitchen for her breakfast.

In the corner of the tool-house was a box half filled with rags. Down among the rags nestled and squirmed and muttered a litter of seven pure-bred collie pups, scarce a fortnight old.

Man-scent and dog-scent filled the air; scaring and disgusting the hesitant Whitefoot. Stark hunger spurred him on. A fleeting black shadow slipped noiselessly swift into the tool-house and then out again.

Through the welter of rain, Whitefoot was making for his mile-distant lair; at top speed; pausing not to glance over his shoulder; straining every muscle to get away from that place of double peril and to his waiting family. No need to waste time in confusing the trail. The sluicing rain was doing that.

Between his teeth the fox carried a squealing and struggling fat collie puppy.

Keen as was his own need for food, he did not pause to devour or even to kill the plump morsel he had snatched up. Nor did his pinpoint teeth so much as prick through the fuzzy fat sides of his prey. Holding the puppy as daintily as a bird dog might retrieve a wounded partridge, he sped on.

At the mouth of the warren, Pitchdark was waiting for him. She had brought her babies out of the death hole; though too late. They lay strewn on the rain-sick ground in front of her. She herself was crouched for shelter in the lee of a rock that stood beside the hole.

Whitefoot dropped the collie pup in front of his mate; and prepared to join her in the banquet. Pitchdark nosed the blind, helpless atom of babyhood; as though trying to make out what it might be.

The puppy, finding himself close to something warm and soft and furry, crept instinctively toward this barrier from the cold and wet which were striking through to the very heart of him. At his forward motion, Pitchdark snarled down at him. But as his poking nose chanced to touch her, the snarl merged suddenly into a croon. With her own sharp nose, she pushed him closer to her and interposed her body between him and the rain.

Whitefoot, the water cascading from his splendid coat, stood dripping and staring. Failing to make any sense of his mate's delay in beginning to devour the breakfast he had brought along at such danger to himself, he took a step forward, his jaws parting for the first mouthful of the feast. Pitchdark growled hideously at him and slashed at his advancing face.

Piqued and amazed at her ungrateful treatment, he hesitated a moment longer; then trotted glumly off into the rain; leaving Pitchdark crooningly nursing the queer substitute for her five dead infants. As he ran, he all but collided with a rain-dazed rabbit that hopped out of a briar clump to avoid him.

Five minutes later he and Pitchdark were lying side by side in the lee of the rock, crunching unctuously the bones of the luckless bunny; while the collie pup feasted as happily in his own fashion as did they, nuzzling deep into the soft hair of his foster-mother's warm underbody.

Why the exposure to rain and cold did not kill the puppy is as much a mystery as why Pitchdark did not kill him. Nevertheless—as is the odd way of one collie pup in twenty—he took no harm from the mile of rainy gallop to which Whitefoot had treated him. More— he throve amain on the milk which had been destined for five fox cubs.

The downpour was followed by weeks of unseasonably dry and warm weather. The porous earth of the warren was dry within a few hours. The lair bed proved as comfortable for the new baby as it was to have been to his luckless predecessors.

By the time May brought the warm nights and the long bright days, the puppy weighed more than twice as much as any fox cub of his age. He had ceased to look like a sleek dun-coloured rat and resembled rather a golden-and-white Teddy Bear.

On the moonlit May nights and in the red dawning and in the soft afterglow, he and his pretty mother would frisk and gambol in the lush young meadow grass around the lair. It was sweet to see the lithe black beauty's complete devotion for her clumsy baby and the jealous care wherewith she guarded him. From the first she was teaching him the cunning caution which is a fox's world-old birthright and which is foreign to a man-owned collie. With his foster-mother's milk and from his foster-mother's example he drank in the secrets of the wild and the fact that man is the dread foe of the beast.

Gaily as the two might play in the moonlit grass, the first distant whiff of man-scent was enough to send Pitchdark scuttling silently into the burrow; driving the shambling pup ahead of her. There the two would lie, noiseless, almost without breathing; while man or dog or both passed by.

This was not the season for hunting foxes. Their pelts were "off-prime"—in no condition for the market. Thus, the pair in the burrow were not sought out nor harried.

Back at the Logan farm there was bewilderment at the puppy's mysterious vanishing. His dam, returning from the kitchen after breakfast, had broken into a growl of sudden wrath and had changed her trot for a handgallop as she neared the tool-shed. Into the shed she had dashed, abristle and growling, then out again, sniffing the earth, casting in ever widening circles, and setting off presently on a trail which the deluging rain wiped out before she could follow it for a hundred yards.

The stolen pup was the only one in the litter which had not been sold or else bespoken. For the Logan collies had a just fame in the region. But that one pup had been set aside by Dick Logan as a future housedog. This because he was the largest and strongest and liveliest of the seven; and because of the unusually wide white ruff which encircled his broad shoulders like a shawl.

Dick had named the youngster "Ruff," because of this adornment. And now he was liked to have no use for the name.

Ruff, meantime, was gaining his education, such as it was, far more quickly than his super-domesticated collie mother and Dick together could have imparted it to him.

By example and by swift punishment in event of disobedience, Pitchdark was teaching him to crouch, flattened and noiseless, at sound or scent of man or of alien beast. She was teaching him to worm his pudgy little body snakelike through grass and undergrowth and to make wise use of every bit of cover. She was teaching him—as foxes have taught their young for a million years— the incredible cunning of her race and the fear of man.

By the time his legs could fairly support him on the briefest of journeys, she was teaching him to stalk game;—to creep up on foolish fieldmice, to confuse and head off young rabbits; and the like. Before he was fairly weaned she made him try his awkward prowess at finishing a rabbit-kill she had begun. With Ruff it was a case of kill or starve. For Pitchdark cut off natural supplies from him a full week earlier than his own gentle mother would have done.

Pitchdark was a born schoolmistress in Nature's grim woodland course of "eat or be eaten." To her stern teachings the puppy brought a brain such as no fox could hope to possess. Ruff was a collie—member of a breed which can assimilate practically any mental or physical teachings, if taught rightly and at an early enough age. Pitchdark was teaching him rightly, if rigidly. Assuredly, too, she was beginning early enough.

To the imparted cunning of the fox, Ruff added the brain of a highly sensitised collie. The combination was a triumph. He learned well-nigh as fast as Pitchdark could teach. If nine-tenths of the things she taught him were as reprehensible as they were needful, he deserved no less credit for his speed in mastering them and for his native ability to add to them.

At an age when his brethren and sisters, back at the farm, were still playing aimlessly around the dooryard, Ruff was grasping the weird secrets of the wild. While they were still at the Teddy Bear stage of appealing helplessness, his fat body was turning lean and supple from raw food and from much exercise and from the nature of that exercise. While they were romping merrily with an old shoe, Ruff was creeping up on fieldmouse nests and on couchant quail, or he was heading off witlessly racing rabbits which his foster-mother drove toward the cul-de-sacs where she had stationed him.

For a pup situated like Ruff, there were two open courses—abnormal thriving or quick starvation. Ruff throve.

By the time he was three months old he weighed nearly eighteen pounds. He was more than a third heavier than Pitchdark, though the silvered black vixen had the appearance of being fully twice his size. A fox is the most deceptive creature on earth, in regard to bulk. Pitchdark, for instance, gave the impression of being as large as any thirty-pound terrier, if of far different build. Yet, stripped of her pelt, her slim carcass would not have weighed eleven pounds. Perhaps it would not have weighed more than ten pounds, for she was not large for her kind.

Before Ruff was six weeks old, Whitefoot had tired of domesticity—especially with so perplexing a canine slant to it—and had deserted his mate and foster-son.

The warm days were coming on. The woods at last were alive with catchable game. The chickens on many a farm were perching out of doors at night. Life was gloriously livable. There seemed no sense in fettering himself to a family, nor for helping to provide for a huge youngster in whom his own interest was purely gastronomical.

More than once Whitefoot had sought to slay and eat the changeling. But ever, at such times, Pitchdark was at him, ravening and raging in defence of her suckling.

Then crept the influx of spring food into the valley and

mountain. There was dinner to be gotten more easily than by battling a ferocious mate for it, a mate who no longer felt even her oldtime lonely comradeship for the dog-fox, and whose every thought and care was for the sprawling puppy. Apart from this, the inherently hated dog-scent on Ruff was a continual irritation to Whitefoot; though maternal care had long since accustomed Pitchdark to it.

Thus on a morning in late April Whitefoot wandered away and neglected to return. His mate was forced to forage for herself and for Ruff. But the task was easy in this new time of food lushness. She did not seem to miss her recreant spouse.

She and Ruff shifted their abode from the burrow whose narrow sides the fast-growing pup could scarce squeeze through. They took up changeable quarters in the hinterland forest. There Ruff's training began in grim earnest.

So the sweet spring and the long drowsy summer wore themselves away. Through the fat months Pitchdark and Ruff abode together; drawn toward each other by the queerly strong tie that so often knits foster-dam and child, in the fourfoot kingdom;—a tie that is prone to be far stronger than that of normal brute mother and offspring.

This chumship now was wholly a thing of choice. For no longer did Ruff depend on the vixen to teach him how to catch his daily bread. True, he profited still by her experience and her abnormal cunning, and he assimilated it and improved on it—as is the way with a collie when he is taught something that catches his bright fancy. But he was self-supporting.

He continued to live with Pitchdark and to travel with her and to hunt with her; not because he needed to, but because he loved her. To this temperamental black-and-silver vixen went out all the loyal devotion and hero-worship and innate protectiveness which a normal collie lavishes on the human who is his god.

Together they roved the mountain, where Pitchdark's technique and craft bagged illimitable game for them. Together on dark nights they scouted the farm-valleys, where Ruff's strength and odd audacity won them access to hencoop after hencoop whose rickety door would have resisted a fox's onslaught.

Twice, Ruff forced his way through the rotting palings of a sheepfold and bore thence to his admiring foster-mother a lamb that was twice as heavy as Pitchdark. Once in open field he fought and outmanœuvred and thrashed a sheep-herding mongrel; dragging off in triumph a half-grown wether.

There were things about Pitchdark the young collie could not

13

understand; just as there were traits of his which baffled her keen wits. To him a grape vineyard was a place whose sole interest centred about any possible field-mouse nests in its mould. An apple orchard had as little significance to him. He would pause and look in questioning surprise as Pitchdark stopped, during their progress through an orchard, to munch happily at a fallen harvest apple; or while she stood daintily on her hindlegs to strip grapevines of their ripening clusters.

The fable of the fox and the sour grapes had its basis in natural history. For the fox, almost alone of carnivora, loves fruit. Ruff cared nothing for it. Few collies do.

Also, he could see no reason for Pitchdark's rapture when they chanced upon the rotting carcasses of animals. True, he felt an æsthetic thrill in rubbing first one shoulder and then the other in such liquescent carrion and then in rolling luxuriously over on his back in it. But it was not good to eat. Ruff knew that. Yet Pitchdark devoured it in delight. On the other hand, when the two came upon a young hawk that had fallen from its pine-top nest, Pitchdark gave one sniff at the broken bird of prey; and then pattered on, leaving it alone. Ruff killed and ate it with relish.

By the first cool days of autumn, Ruff stood twenty-four inches at the shoulder. He would have tipped the scales at a fraction above fifty pounds. His gold-red winter coat was beginning to come in, luxuriantly and with a sheen such as only the pelt of a forest-dweller can boast. His young chest was deep. His shoulders were broad and sinewy. His build was that of a wild beast; not of a domesticated dog. Diet and tremendous exercise and his mode of life had wrought that vast difference.

He had the noiselessly padding gait and the furtive air of a fox. Mentally and morally he was a fox; plus the keener and finer brain of a collie. His dark and deepset eyes had the glint of the wild, rather than the straight-forward gaze of a collie. Yet those eyes were a dog's and not a fox's. A fox has the eye of a cat, not of a dog. The iris is not round, but is long and slitted, like a cat's. In bright sunlight it closes to a vertical line, and does not contract to a tiny circle, like dog's or man's.

Nor did Ruff have the long and couchant hindlegs and short catlike forelegs of Pitchdark. His were the honestly sturdy legs and sturdy pads of a collie.

The wolf is the dog's brother. They be of one blood. They can and do mate as readily as dog and dog. Dog and fox are far different. Their cousinship is remote. Their physique is remoter;—too remote to permit of blending. There is almost as much of the cat as of the

14

dog in a fox's cosmos;—too much of it to permit of interbreeding with the cat-detesting dog.

Yet Ruff and Pitchdark were loving pals. They profited materially from their association; so far as food-getting went. They were inseparable comrades, through the fat summer and autumn and in the lean winter which followed.

In the bitter weather, when rabbits were few and when most birds had flown south and when rodents were holed in, it was young Ruff whose daring and strength enabled them to snatch fawns from snow-lined deer-yards in the mountain creases and to raid sheepfolds and rip through flimsy hencoop doors. He kept them alive and he kept them in good condition. Daily he grew larger and stronger and wilier.

At a year, he weighed a full sixty pounds; and he had the strength and uncanny quickness of a tiger-cat. It was he now who led; while Pitchdark followed in meek adoration. Such foxes as they chanced to meet fled in sullen terror before the collie's assault. Ruff did not like foxes.

The next autumn brought forth the hunters. A few city folk and farm-boys ranged the hills with fowling piece and with or without bird dog or rabbit hound. These novices were ridiculously easy for Ruff and Pitchdark to avoid. They offered still less menace to Whitefoot ranging in solitary comfort on the thither side of the mountain wall.

But the real hunters of the region were a more serious obstacle to smug comfort and to safety. They were lanky or stumpy men in woolly old clothes and accompanied by businesslike hounds. These men did not bother with mere sport or pot hunting. Red fox pelts brought this year $11.50 each, uncured, from the wholesaler down at Heckettville. Fox hunting was a recognised form of livelihood here in the upland valley district.

It was not like quail shooting or other sport open to any amateur. It was an art. It called for craft and for experience and for a rudimentary knowledge of the habits of foxes and for perfect marksmanship. Also it required the aid of a well-trained foxhound;—not the type of foxhound the pink coats trail after, in conventional hunting fields—not the spruce foxhound on exhibition at dogshows—but rangy and stringy and wise and tireless dogs of dubious pedigree but vast fox-sense.

A veteran hunter with a good hound, in that part of the country and in those days, could readily pay the year's taxes and improvements on his farm by the fox-pelts he was able to secure in a single month's roaming of the hills. Wherefore, now that the year's farmwork was done, these few experts began their season of lucrative and sportless sport.

Time and again some gaunt and sad-faced hound, that fall, hit Pitchdark's confused trail; only to veer from it presently when his nostrils caught the unmistakable dog-scent along with it. Still oftener did a hound cling tenaciously to that trail; only to be outwitted by the vixen's cleverer manœuvres.

Pitchdark had as much genius for eluding pursuit as for climbing unclimbable fences. There are such foxes.

In these retreats from pursuing hounds it was she who took up afresh the leadership she had laid down. Ruff followed her, implicitly, in her many mazelike twists and doublings. At first he followed, blindly. But gradually he began to get the hang of it, and to devise collie improvements on the hide-and-seek game.

He and she were alone in their wanderings; especially since the hunting season forced them higher among the almost inaccessible peaks of the range. Foxes that crossed their path or happened to sight or scent them fled as ever in terror at the dog-smell.

In midwinter, the day after a "tracking snow" had fallen, one Jeffreys Holt, an aged fox-hunter, tramping home with his tired hound at his heels, chanced upon an incredible sight.

An animal rounded a bend of rock on a hillside perhaps a hundred yards in front of him; and stood there, stockstill, for a few seconds, sharply outlined against the snow. Then, as Holt stared slackjawed, the creature oozed from sight into a crevice. Holt plunged ahead, urging his weary hound to the chase. But by the time he reached the crevice there was no sign of the quarry.

The cleft led through to an opening on the far side of a rocky outcrop. Thence a hundred-yard rib of rock jutted above the snow. Along this, presumably, had the prey fled; for there were no further marks of him in the whiteness. Holt cast his dog futilely upon the trail. He studied the footprints in the snow at the point where first the beast had been standing. Then he plodded home.

Whitefoot, from the safety of another double-entry rock-lair, a furlong away, watched him depart. Long immunity had made the big dog-fox overbold. Yet this was the first time human eyes had focused on him for two years.

At the store, that night, Rance Venner glanced up from his task of ordering supplies for the Stippled Silver Kennels and listened with sudden interest to the harangue of an oldster among the group around the stove.

"I'm telling you," Holt was insisting, in reply to a doubter,

16

"I'm telling you I saw him as plain as I see you. Jet black he was, only his tailtip was white, and one of his hindfeet; and there was shiny grey hairs sticking out from his shoulders and over his eyebrows. He—"

"Somebody's black dog, most likely," suggested the doubter.

"Dog nothing!" snorted Holt. "I've killed too many foxes not to know 'em from dogs. This was a fox. A reg'lar ol' he-one. A corker. And I'm telling you he was coal-black; all but the tip of his tail and them hairs sprinkled all over his mask and—"

"Well," soothed the doubter, seeking to calm Holt's vexed vehemence, "I'm not saying there mayn't be black foxes with white tails and white hindfeet and grey masks. For all I know, there's maybe foxes that's bright green and foxes that's red-white-and-blue, or speckled with pink. There may be. Only nobody's ever seen 'em. Any more'n anybody's ever seen a black-and-white-and-grey one, till you seen that one to-day, Jeff. I—"

Rance Venner came into the circle of disputants. He did not mingle with the folk of this village, six miles from his fox-farm. This was his first visit to the store. The emporium nearest his home had burned down, that week. Hence his need to go farther afield for supplies.

"You say you saw a silver fox?" he asked excitedly, confronting Holt.

Holt stared truculently at him; suspecting further banter and not relishing it from a stranger.

"Nope," solemnly spoke up the doubter. "Not silver. Rainbow-colour, with a streak of this here radium you've likely heard tell of. Jeff Holt don't see queer things, often. But when he does, he sure sees 'em plenty vivid."

"My name is Venner," went on Rance, still addressing Holt. "My brother and I run the Stippled Silver Fox Farm, up above Croziers. Two years ago a couple of our silver foxes got loose on us. They—"

"Sure they wasn't di'mond foxes?" asked the doubter, politely.

The audience snickered at this scintillant flash of native wit. But Rance went on, unheeding. Briefly, he explained the appearance and general nature and value of silver foxes; and expanded upon the loss of the two that had escaped from his kennel.

His oration gained scant personal interest; until he made a cash offer of $75 to any one who would bring him Whitefoot's or Pitchdark's pelt in good condition. He made an offer of $125 for either fox if captured alive and undamaged.

At this point incredulity reached its climax among his hearers.

17

But when Venner pulled twenty-five dollars from his hip pocket and deposited it with the postmaster-storekeeper in evidence of good faith, the sight of real money caused a wholesale conversion.

This conversion became rockbound conviction when, next night, Holt returned from a call upon the wholesale pelt-buyer at Heckettville, fifteen miles away.

"Say!" reported Holt, to the group of idling men at the stoveside. "That Venner cuss ain't loony, after all. Gannett told me all about them silver foxes. They're true, all right. Showed me a picture of one. The spitting image of the one I seen. Gave me this circ'lar to prove it. It was sent to him by the gov'ment or by some sort of association. Listen here."

Drawing out a folder, he began to read at random:

"Some silver foxes are cheap at $1,000.... If every silver fox in the world should be pelted in November or December, when the fur is prime, they could all be disposed of in a city the size of New York, in less than a week, at a fab—at a fab'lous sum."

Impressively and for the most part taking the more unfamiliar words in his stride, Jeffreys Holt continued to read. Nor did he cease until he had made his eager audience acquainted with every line of the folder, including the printer's name and address in the lozenge at the foot of the fourth page.

Next morning all available fox traps for some miles around were on duty in the woods and among the hilltop rock-barrens. Every man who understood the first thing about fox hunting was abroad with gun and dog, as well as local wealth-seekers to whom the fine art of tracking foxes was merely a thing of hearsay. In that meagre community and in that meagre time of a meagre year, the lure of $75, to say nothing of $125, was irresistible. The village went afield.

Rance Venner and his brother were among the hunters, they and their little mixed-blood foxhound, Ruby.

Before dawn, Ruff and Pitchdark caught the distant signs of the chase, and they denned in, far among the peak rocks, for the day. At that, the chase might perhaps have neared their lofty eyrie before sunset, but for Whitefoot.

The big dog-fox had enjoyed long immunity from harm. He lacked Pitchdark's super-caution. His adventure with man and dog, two days earlier, had resulted in no harm to himself. With entire ease he had blurred pursuit. Seeking rabbits again, in the clefts of the same rockridge, at sunrise on this day of universal hunting, he heard hounds baying futilely in far quarters of the valley and foothills below him.

Instead of denning in, as had his former mate and Ruff, he went on with his own hunt. Lacking a confederate like the collie to help him find food which was beyond his own vulpine powers to capture or slay, Whitefoot had begun to feel the pinch of winter-hunger. Unappeasable appetite made him take chances from which the vixen would have recoiled.

For example, the sound and smell of the distant hunt, this morning, did not send him to cover. All autumn and early winter he had been hearing such far-off sounds, had been catching the man-and-dog scent. Never had he come to harm from any of it. He had been able to keep out of its way. Until that afternoon when Holt chanced upon him, no human eye had seen him. And even then there had been no trouble about getting away clean.

There were rabbits hiding in these clefts and crevices along the ridge-side. Whitefoot could smell them. With luck he might be able to stampede one of them into a cul-de-sac cranny big enough to admit his own slim body.

An empty and gnawing stomach urged him on. It urged him on, even after he caught the scent of human footprints which had passed that way, not an hour agone. It urged him on, even when, in a cranny, he came upon a contrivance of wood and iron which fairly reeked of human touch. The thing reeked of something else—of an excessively dead chicken which lay just beyond it in the cleft.

Too crafty to go past such a man-made and man-scented contrivance, yet Whitefoot felt his mouth water at the ancient odour of the chicken. He craved it beyond anything. Detouring the top of the ridge, he entered the cleft from the other side. No visible object of man's workmanship checked him here or stood between him and the tempting food. Of course the man-scent was as strong here as at the opposite end. But the morning wind was shifting through the cleft, bearing the reek with it.

Cautiously the half-starved fox padded forward through the drift of dead leaves toward the chicken which itself was half buried in leafage. His jaws closed on it.

As he backed out with his treasure-trove, steel jaws closed on his left forefoot.

An hour later, Rance Venner and Holt climbed the ridge to visit the former's newfangled patent fox-trap. In the centre of a patch of bloody trampled snow lay a magnificent silver fox; moveless, his eyes rolled back; his teeth curled away from his upper jaw. Limp and pitifully still he lay.

Venner ran forward with a cry of joy and knelt to unfasten the trap jaws from the lifeless creature's paw.

"It's our King Whitefoot II!" he exulted, laying the supine body in his lap and smoothing the rumpled glory of pelt. "But I can't figure why he's dead. Maybe the shock killed him, or else he broke a blood-vessel in his brain trying to tear loose. He—"

The rambling conjecture ended in a hoot of pain. There was an indescribably swift whirl of the inert black body. Rance Venner's thumb received a lightning bite from teeth which scraped sickeningly into its very bone. Whitefoot was flying like mad for the nearest available rock-cranny.

Venner once more was increasing his knowledge of fox-character. Apart from enacting prodigies at digging and at climbing, it appeared now that foxes, in emergency, understood to perfection the trick of playing dead.

Away flashed Whitefoot, his lacerated forepaw marring his speed not at all. Jeffreys Holt was an old enough huntsman to act on sheer instinct. Through no conscious volition of his own he whipped to his shoulder the gun that had hung idle in his grasp while he watched Rance open the trap. Taking snap aim, he pulled trigger.

Whitefoot did not stop at once his panic flight. He continued it for two yards longer; rolling over and over like a mechanical toy, before thumping against the rock-side, stone dead.

"There's another good stunt we done, in getting that ol' feller," remarked Holt, ten minutes later, as he and Venner made their way downhill with their prize. "I'll bet my share of his pelt he's the fox that's been working the hencoops all along the valley, this winter. He's a whooping big cuss. And no common-size fox could 'a busted in the coop doors like he did at a couple of places. Now that we got the fox, I s'pose it's up to us to get the wolf."

"What wolf?" mumbled Venner, still sucking his bitten thumb.

"Why, the one the Grange reward is out for, of course," answered Holt in surprise at such ignorance. "First wolf that's been in this section in thutty years or more. He's been at sheepfolds, all over. At hencoops, too. First-off folks thought maybe it was a stray cur. But no dog c'd do the smart wolf-stunts that feller's done. Pizen-shy and trap-wise. It's a wolf, all right, all right."

The store was jammed, for two hours or more, that evening, by folk who came to stare at the wonder-fox. Next day and the next the whole community was out in quest of the priceless vixen.

All the second day, after a night of successful forage, Ruff and Pitchdark denned amid the rocks of their peak. At nightfall they fared forth again, as usual. But as they were padding contentedly back to their safe eyrie at grey dawn, Pitchdark failed to note a deadfall which had been placed in a hillside gully three months earlier.

20

Going back and forth—always of course by different routes—during the past three days, she and Ruff had scented and avoided a score of shrewdly-laid traps scattered here and there. But this clumsy deadfall had been in place since November, when a farm lad had set it and then forgotten all about it. Rains and snow and winds had rubbed it clean of any vestige of man-scent. It seemed nothing but a fallen log propped against a tree-trunk.

By way of a short cut, Pitchdark ran under it.

There was a thump, followed at once by an astounded yell. The vixen, flattened out, lay whimpering under the tumbled log.

Ruff was trotting along; a yard or so behind her. The fall of the log had made him spring instinctively sideways. Now he went over to where Pitchdark lay moaning and writhing. Tenderly he sniffed at her; then he walked around the log and her pinioned body. In another second he was at work clawing and shoving at the weight that imprisoned her.

The log was too light for its purpose. Also the boy who made and set the trap was a novice. The end of the log had come to rest on a knot of wood near the tree base. Ruff's weight and applied strength set it a-rolling. Off from the vixen it bumped; while she cried out again in agony.

Ruff turned to greet her as she should leap joyously to her feet. But she did not leap. The impact of the falling log had injured her spine. The best she could do was to crawl painfully along, stomach to the ground; whining with pain at every step. Her hindlegs sagged useless. Her forepaws made all the progress.

Yet she was a gallant sufferer. Keenly aware that she was in no condition to face or flee any possible dangers of the open, she made pluckily for the eyrie on the distant peak. The great collie slackened his pace to hers. At a windfall, too high for her to clamber over, he caught her gently by the nape of the neck with his mighty jaws and scrambled over the impediment, carrying her with him.

Thus, at snail-pace, they made their way homeward; the collie close beside his crippled chum; quivering from head to foot in distress as now and then the pain forced from her a sharp outcry.

Dawn deepened into daylight. Up came the winter sun, shouldering its sulky way through dun horizon mists. The day was on. And Ruff and Pitchdark were not yet within a mile of their hiding place.

The last mile promised to be the worst mile; rising as it did, almost precipice-like, to the summit; and strewn with boulder and rift. To the light-footed pair, such a clamber had ever been childishly easy. Now it threatened to be one long torment to the vixen.

No longer, since the accident, did they seek as usual to confuse or obliterate their homeward trail. There was no question now of wasting a step or of delaying the needful moment of safety.

Then, as they came to a ten-foot cliff, at the base of the peak's last stiff climb, they halted and looked miserably upward. Along the face of this rock wall a narrow rudimentary trail ran, from bottom to top; a widened rock-fissure. The fox and the collie were wont to take it almost at a bound.

But now there was no question of bounding. Nor was the collie able to navigate the tricky climb with Pitchdark suspended from his jaws. It was not a matter of weight but of leverage and of balance. He had sense enough to know that.

For the past half-mile he had been carrying the vixen, her helpless hindlegs dragging along the ground. Very tenderly, by the nape of the neck, he had borne her along. Yet the wrenching motion had forced cries from her, so that once and again he had set her down and stared in pitiful sorrow at her.

Now, Pitchdark took matters into her own hands. At the base of the cliff was an alcove niche of rock, perhaps two feet deep and eighteen inches wide; roofed over by a slant of half-fallen stone. It was bedded with dead leaves. There were worse holes into which to crawl to die, than was this natural den. Into it, painfully, wearily, the vixen dragged her racked body. There she laid herself down on the leaf-couch; spent and in torture. She had come to the end of her journey; though still a mile on the hither side of the den where she and Ruff were wont to hide.

It was no hiding place, no safe refuge, this niche of rock wherein she lay. But it was the best substitute. Panting, she settled down to bear her anguish as best she might. Above her, at the opening of the niche, stood the heartsick dog that loved her.

Puzzled, miserable, tormented, he stood there. At times he would bend down to lick the sufferer, crooning softly to her. But she gave him scant heed.

A rabbit scuttled across the snowy open space in front of the cliff. With a dash, Ruff was after him. A few rods away the chase ended in a reddened swirl of the snow. Back to Pitchdark trotted Ruff, the rabbit in his mouth. He laid the offering in front of her. But she was past eating or so much as noticing food.

Then, as he watched her, his deepset dark eyes sick with pity and grief, he stiffened to attention; and his lip curled away from his curving white teeth. The morning breeze bore to him a scent and a sound that had but one meaning.

The scent was of dogs. The sound was of multiple baying.

Instinctively he glanced at the cliff-trail—the trail he could surmount so quickly and easily, to the safety of the peak's upper reaches. Then his unhappy gaze fell on Pitchdark. The baying and the odour had reached her even more keenly than it had reached Ruff. She read it aright; and the realisation brought her out of the pain-daze into which she had fallen. She tried to get to her feet. Failing, she fell to whimpering softly.

Once she peered up, questioningly, at Ruff. The big collie was standing in front of the niche, shielding it with his strong body. His head was high and his eye had the look of eagles. Gone from his expression was the furtiveness of the wild. In this crisis he was all collie. The sun blazed on his flaming red-gold coat and his snowy mass of ruff and frill. Every muscle was tense. Every faculty was alert.

Zeb Harlow knew nothing about fox-hunting. Indeed, he knew little enough about anything. But at the store conclave, the preceding night, his fancy had been fired by tales of the silver foxhunt. He had an inspiration.

Before daybreak he was abroad; gun in hand. Going from one sleeping neighbour's to another's, he loosed and took along with him no fewer than five chained foxhounds.

The dogs all knew him well enough to let him handle them. There was not one of the five that would not have followed anybody who carried a gun. So his one-man hunt was organised. He and the five hounds made for the ridge where, two days before, Whitefoot had been caught.

From reading nature-faked tales of rattlesnakes, Zeb argued that the slain fox's mate would be haunting the scene of her spouse's death. It was a pretty theory; as pretty as it was asinine. Like many another wholly idiotic premise it led to large results—of a sort.

As Zeb was traversing a wooded gully on the way to the ridge, the foremost hound gave tongue. The pack had come to the spot where Pitchdark had been crippled. From that point a blind mongrel puppy could have followed the pungent trail.

Oblivious of Harlow, for whom they had all a dog's amusedly tolerant contempt for an inefficient human leader, the quintet swept away on the track. Zeb made shift to follow as best he could. Not being a woodsman, his progress was slow.

Up the gully they roared and out into the hillside birch woods beyond and thence to the patch of broken ground over which Ruff had carried Pitchdark so tenderly. The scent was rankly strong now. It was breast-high. No longer was there need to work with nostrils to earth. The dragging hindfeet of the vixen were easier to follow than an aniseed lure.

Out into the cleared space they swung—the clearing with the ten-foot cliff behind it. There, not fifty yards in front of them, clearly visible between the braced legs of a shimmering gold-and-white collie on guard at the niche opening, crouched their prey.

Deliriously they rushed to the kill.

The kill was there. But so was the killer.

Perhaps there are two foxhounds on earth which together can down a normal collie. Assuredly there is no one foxhound that can hope to achieve the deed. Most assuredly such a hound was not the half-breed black-and-yellow leader of that impromptu pack.

The black-and-yellow made for the niche, a clean dozen lengths ahead of his nearest follower. Blind to all but the lust of slaughter, he dived between the braced legs of the movelessly-waiting collie, and struck for the cowering vixen.

Ruff drove downward at him as the hound dived. The collie's terrible jaws clamped shut behind the base of the leader's skull. The aim, made accurate by a thousand snaps at fleeing rabbits and rising birds, was flawless. The jaws had been strengthened past normal by the daily grinding of bony food.

Ruff tossed high his head. The black-and-yellow was flung in air and fell back amid his onrushing fellows; his neck broken, his spinal cord severed.

But that was Ruff's last opportunity for individual fighting. The four following hounds were upon him; in one solid battling mass. Noting their leader's fate they did not make the error of trying to jostle past to the vixen. Instead, they sought to clear the way by flinging themselves ravenously on her solitary guard.

The rest was horror.

There was no scope for scientific fighting or for craft. The four fastened upon the collie, in murderous unison. They might more wisely have fastened upon a hornet-nest.

Down, under their avalanche of weight went Ruff; battling as he fell. But a collie down is not a collie beaten. As he fell, he slashed to the bone the nearest gaunt shoulder. By the time he had struck ground on his back, he lunged upward for one flying spotted hindleg that chanced to flounder nearest to his jaws. The fighting tricks of his long-ago wolf ancestors came to him in his hour of stress. Catching the leg midway between hock and body he gave a sidewise wrench to it that wellnigh heaved off the pack that piled upon him. The possessor of the spotted hindleg screeched aloud and gave back, tumbling out of the ruck with a fractured and useless limb.

Up from the tangle of fighting hounds arose Ruff, his golden coat a-smear with blood. High he reared above the surrounding heads. Slashing, tearing, dodging, wheeling, he fought clear of his mangled foes.

For an instant, as they gathered their force for a new charge at this tigerlike adversary, the great collie stood clear of them all. A single bound would have carried him to the cliff trail. Thence, to its top would have been a climb of less than half a second. At the summit he could have fought back an army of dogs or he could have made his escape to the fastnesses beyond. Never was there a foxhound that could keep pace with a racing collie.

The coast was clear, if only for an instant. There was time—just time—for the leap. Ruff made the leap.

But he did not make it in the direction of the inviting trail. Instead, he sprang back again in front of the trembling vixen as she crouched in her niche.

A fox would have fled. So would any creature of the wild. But no longer was Ruff a creature of the wild. In his supreme moment he was all collie.

Whirling to face his oncoming enemies he took his stand. And there the charge of the hounds crashed into him.

By footwork, by dodging, by leading his foes into a chase where they should string out, he could have conquered them. But this he dared not do. He knew well what must befall Pitchdark the moment he should leave the niche unguarded. So he stood where he was; and went down once more under the rush.

There were but three opponents atop him, this time. The spotted hound was out of the fight, with a crunched leg and a craven heart. Nor were any of the three others unmarked by slash or nip or tear.

Now, as Ruff fell he pulled one of the three down with him; his awful fangs busy at the hound's throat. A second of the trio rolled over with them; the forequarters of his inverted body sprawled within the niche. While he bit and roared at the fast-rolling Ruff, the vixen saw her chance. Darting her head forward, she set her needle teeth deep in the hound's throat. Instantly, seared by the hurt, he was atop her; ripping away at her unprotected back; tearing it to ribbons. But, with death upon her and the rear half of her paralysed, she did not abate the merciless grinding at the hound's throat. Presently, the needle teeth found their goal.

Ruff was up again; one of his assailants gasping out his life beneath him; the other with Pitchdark clinging in death to his throat. Torn and bleeding and panting as he was, Ruff flew at the fourth dog; the only one of the five still in fighting condition.

Before that one-to-one onset the mongrel hound's heart went

back on him. He turned and fled; but not before Ruff's madly twisting jaws had lamed him for life.

The battle was fought and won. Of the five hounds, one lay dead; two more were dying, a fourth was lying helpless with a crunched hindleg. The fifth was in limping flight.

The young collie staggered, then righted himself. Crossing to Pitchdark, he bent painfully down and licked her face—the face whose teeth were locked in her oppressor's throat.

Never now would that glorious pelt sell for hundreds of dollars; or even for hundreds of cents. The dying hound had seen to that. So had the dog now limping away. This latter had taken advantage of Ruff's preoccupation with his two fellows, as they rolled in the snow, to tear destructively at the silken coat as the vixen's teeth were finding their way to his comrade's jugular.

Crooning, licking, Ruff sought to make his loved little foster-mother awaken. Then he lifted his head and wheeled wearily about to face a new intruder.

Across the snow toward him was clumping a slack-faced man who gripped in both hands a cocked gun and who was shouting foolishly in his excitement. Zeb Harlow had caught up to the hunt at last.

Ruff had not been so near to any human since he was a fortnight old. The carefully-taught lessons of Pitchdark warned him to turn and flee. The cliff trail was still open to him. But into the brain that was once again all collie there seeped a queer sensation the big dog could not analyse.

His dear little comrade was dead. Without her the old life would be empty. His was the collie heritage—the stark need for comradeship; coupled with the unconscious craving to be owned by man and to give his devotion to man, his god.

Still unable to analyse his own unwonted feelings, Ruff bent again and licked Pitchdark's dead face. Then, hesitant, he took a step toward the stormily advancing Harlow. He took another irresolute step; paused again and wagged his plumy tail.

"Attacked me, he did!" bragged Zeb Harlow, that night at the store. "Come straight for me, like he was going to eat me alive. But I stopped him, all right, all right. I stood my ground. After the second step he took, I let him have both bar'ls. You saw for yourselves what he looked like after he tried to tackle ME."

TWO

The Coming of Lad

In the mile-away village of Hampton, there had been a veritable epidemic of burglaries—ranging from the theft of a brand-new ash-can from the steps of the Methodist chapel to the ravaging of Mrs. Blauvelt's whole lineful of clothes, on a washday dusk.

Up the Valley and down it, from Tuxedo to Ridgewood, there had been a half-score robberies of a very different order—depredations wrought, manifestly, by professionals; thieves whose motor cars served the twentieth century purpose of such historic steeds as Dick Turpin's Black Bess and Jack Shepard's Ranter. These thefts were in the line of jewelry and the like; and were as daringly wrought as were the modest local operators' raids on ash-can and laundry.

It is the easiest thing in the world to stir humankind's ever-tense burglar-nerves into hysterical jangling. In house after house, for miles of the peaceful North Jersey region, old pistols were cleaned and loaded; window fastenings and door-locks were inspected and new hiding-places found for portable family treasures.

Across the lake from the village, and down the Valley from a dozen country homes, seeped the tide of precautions. And it swirled at last around the Place,—a thirty-acre homestead, isolated and sweet, whose grounds ran from highway to lake; and whose wisteria-clad grey house drowsed among big oaks midway between road and water; a furlong or more distant from either.

The Place's family dog,—a pointer,—had died, rich in years and honour. And the new peril of burglary made it highly needful to choose a successor for him.

The Master talked of buying a whalebone-and-steel-and-snow bull terrier, or a more formidable if more greedy Great Dane. But the Mistress wanted a collie. So they compromised by getting the collie.

He reached the Place in a crampy and smelly crate; preceded by a long envelope containing an intricate and imposing pedigree. The burglary-preventing problem seemed solved.

But when the crate was opened and its occupant stepped gravely forth, on the Place's veranda, the problem was revived.

27

All the Master and the Mistress had known about the newcomer,—apart from his price and his lofty lineage,—was that his breeder had named him "Lad."

From these meagre facts they had somehow built up a picture of a huge and grimly ferocious animal that should be a terror to all intruders and that might in time be induced to make friends with the Place's vouched-for occupants. In view of this, they had had a stout kennel made and to it they had affixed with double staples a chain strong enough to restrain a bull.

(It may as well be said here that never in all the sixteen years of his beautiful life did Lad occupy that or any other kennel nor wear that or any other chain.)

Even the crate which brought the new dog to the Place failed somehow to destroy the illusion of size and fierceness. But, the moment the crate door was opened the delusion was wrecked by Lad himself.

Out on to the porch he walked. The ramshackle crate behind him had a ridiculous air of a chrysalis from which some bright thing had departed. For a shaft of sunlight was shimmering athwart the veranda floor. And into the middle of the warm bar of radiance Laddie stepped,—and stood.

His fluffy puppy-coat of wavy mahogany-and-white caught a million sunbeams, reflecting them back in tawny-orange glints and in a dazzle as of snow. His forepaws were absurdly small, even for a puppy's. Above them the ridging of the stocky leg-bones gave as clear promise of mighty size and strength as did the amazingly deep little chest and square shoulders.

Here one day would stand a giant among dogs, powerful as a timber-wolf, lithe as a cat, as dangerous to foes as an angry tiger; a dog without fear or treachery; a dog of uncanny brain and great lovingly loyal heart and, withal, a dancing sense of fun. A dog with a soul.

All this, any canine physiologist might have read from the compact frame, the proud head-carriage, the smoulder in the deep-set sorrowful dark eyes. To the casual observer, he was but a beautiful and appealing and wonderfully cuddleable bunch of puppyhood.

Lad's dark eyes swept the porch, the soft swelling green of the lawn, the flash of fire-blue lake among the trees below. Then, he deigned to look at the group of humans at one side of him. Gravely, impersonally, he surveyed them; not at all cowed or strange in his new surroundings; courteously inquisitive as to the twist of luck that had set him down here and as to the people who, presumably, were to be his future companions.

28

Perhaps the stout little heart quivered just a bit, if memory went back to his home kennel and to the rowdy throng of brothers and sisters and, most of all, to the soft furry mother against whose side he had nestled every night since he was born. But if so, Lad was too valiant to show homesickness by so much as a whimper. And, assuredly, this House of Peace was infinitely better than the miserable crate wherein he had spent twenty horrible and jouncing and smelly and noisy hours.

From one to another of the group strayed the level sorrowful gaze. After the swift inspection, Laddie's eyes rested again on the Mistress. For an instant, he stood, looking at her, in that mildly polite curiosity which held no hint of personal interest.

Then, all at once, his plumy tail began to wave. Into his sad eyes sprang a flicker of warm friendliness. Unbidden—oblivious of every one else—he trotted across to where the Mistress sat. He put one tiny white paw in her lap; and stood thus, looking up lovingly into her face, tail awag, eyes shining.

"There's no question whose dog he's going to be," laughed the Master. "He's elected you,—by acclamation."

The Mistress caught up into her arms the half-grown youngster, petting his silken head, running her white fingers through his shining mahogany coat; making crooning little friendly noises to him. Lad forgot he was a dignified and stately pocket-edition of a collie. Under this spell, he changed in a second to an excessively loving and nestling and adoring puppy.

"Just the same," interposed the Master, "we've been stung. I wanted a dog to guard the Place and to be a menace to burglars and all that sort of thing. And they've sent us a Teddy-Bear. I think I'll ship him back and get a grown one. What sort of use is—?"

"He is going to be all those things," eagerly prophesied the Mistress. "And a hundred more. See how he loves to have me pet him! And,—look—he's learned, already, to shake hands, and—"

"Fine!" applauded the Master. "So when it comes our turn to be visited by this motor-Raffles, the puppy will shake hands with him, and register love of petting; and the burly marauder will be so touched by Lad's friendliness that he'll not only spare our house but lead an upright life ever after. I—"

"Don't send him back!" she pleaded. "He'll grow up, soon, and—"

"And if only the courteous burglars will wait till he's a couple of years old," suggested the Master, "he—"

Set gently on the floor by the Mistress, Laddie had crossed to where the Master stood. The man, glancing down, met the puppy's

29

gaze. For an instant he scowled at the miniature watchdog, so ludicrously different from the ferocious brute he had expected. Then,—for some queer reason,—he stooped and ran his hand roughly over the tawny coat, letting it rest at last on the shapely head that did not flinch or wriggle at his touch.

"All right," he decreed. "Let him stay. He'll be an amusing pet for you, anyhow. And his eye has the true thoroughbred expression,—'the look of eagles.' He may amount to something after all. Let him stay. We'll take a chance on burglars."

So it was that Lad came to the Place. So it was that he demanded and received due welcome;—which was ever Lad's way. The Master had been right about the pup's proving "an amusing pet," for the Mistress. From that first hour, Lad was never willingly out of her sight. He had adopted her. The Master, too,—in only a little lesser wholeheartedness,—he adopted. Toward the rest of the world, from the first, he was friendly but more or less indifferent.

Almost at once, his owners noted an odd trait in the dog's nature. He would of course get into any or all of the thousand mischief-scrapes which are the heritage of puppies. But, a single reproof was enough to cure him forever of the particular form of mischief which had just been chidden. He was one of those rare dogs that learn the Law by instinct; and that remember for all time a command or a prohibition once given them.

For example:—On his second day at the Place, he made a furious rush at a neurotic mother hen and her golden convoy of chicks. The Mistress,—luckily for all concerned,—was within call. At her sharp summons the puppy wheeled, midway in his charge, and trotted back to her. Severely, yet trying not to laugh at his worried aspect, she scolded Lad for his misdeed.

An hour later, as Lad was scampering ahead of her, past the stables, they rounded a corner and came flush upon the same nerve-wrecked hen and her brood. Lad halted in his scamper, with a suddenness that made him skid. Then, walking as though on eggs, he made an idiotically wide circle about the feathered dam and her silly chicks. Never thereafter did he assail any of the Place's fowls.

It was the same, when he sprang up merrily at a line of laundry, flapping in alluring invitation from the drying ground lines. A single word of rebuke,—and thenceforth the family wash was safe from him.

And so on with the myriad perplexing "Don'ts" which spatter the career of a fun-loving collie pup. Versed in the patience-fraying ways of pups in general, the Mistress and the Master marvelled and bragged and praised.

All day and every day, life was a delight to the little dog. He had friends, everywhere, willing to romp with him. He had squirrels to chase, among the oaks. He had the lake to splash ecstatically in. He had all he wanted to eat; and he had all the petting his hungry little heart could crave.

He was even allowed, with certain restrictions, to come into the mysterious house itself. Nor, after one defiant bark at a leopardskin rug, did he molest anything therein. In the house, too, he found a genuine cave:—a wonderful place to lie and watch the world at large, and to stay cool in and to pretend he was a wolf. The cave was the deep space beneath the piano in the music room. It seemed to have a peculiar charm to Lad. To the end of his days, by the way, this cave was his chosen resting place. Nor, in his lifetime, did any other dog set foot therein.

So much for "all day and every day." But the nights were different.

Lad hated the nights. In the first place, everybody went to bed and left him alone. In the second, his hard-hearted owners made him sleep on a fluffy rug in a corner of the veranda instead of in his delectable piano-cave. Moreover, there was no food at night. And there was nobody to play with or to go for walks with or to listen to. There was nothing but gloom and silence and dulness.

When a puppy takes fifty cat-naps in the course of the day, he cannot always be expected to sleep the night through. It is too much to ask. And Lad's waking hours at night were times of desolation and of utter boredom. True, he might have consoled himself, as does many a lesser pup, with voicing his woes in a series of melancholy howls. That, in time, would have drawn plenty of human attention to the lonely youngster; even if the attention were not wholly flattering.

But Lad did not belong to the howling type. When he was unhappy, he waxed silence. And his sorrowful eyes took on a deeper woe. By the way, if there is anything more sorrowful than the eyes of a collie pup that has never known sorrow, I have yet to see it.

No, Lad could not howl. And he could not hunt for squirrels. For these enemies of his were not content with the unsportsmanliness of climbing out of his reach in the daytime, when he chased them; but they added to their sins by joining the rest of the world,—except Lad,—in sleeping all night. Even the lake that was so friendly by day was a chilly and forbidding playfellow on the cool North Jersey nights.

There was nothing for a poor lonely pup to do but stretch out on his rug and stare in unhappy silence up the driveway, in the

31

impossible hope that some one might happen along through the darkness to play with him.

At such an hour and in such lonesomeness, Lad would gladly have tossed aside all prejudices of caste,—and all his natural dislikes,—and would have frolicked in mad joy with the veriest stranger. Anything was better than this drear solitude throughout the million hours before the first of the maids should be stirring or the first of the farmhands report for work. Yes, night was a disgusting time; and it had not one single redeeming trait for the puppy.

Lad was not even consoled by the knowledge that he was guarding the slumbrous house. He was not guarding it. He had not the very remotest idea what it meant to be a watchdog. In all his five months he had never learned that there is unfriendliness in the world; or that there is anything to guard a house against.

True, it was instinctive with him to bark when people came down the drive, or appeared at the gates without warning. But more than once the Master had bidden him be silent when a rackety puppy salvo of barking had broken in on the arrival of some guest. And Lad was still in perplexed doubt as to whether barking was something forbidden or merely limited.

One night,—a solemn, black, breathless August night, when half-visible heat lightning turned the murk of the western horizon to pulses of dirty sulphur,—Lad awoke from a fitful dream of chasing squirrels which had never learned to climb.

He sat up on his rug, blinking around through the gloom in the half hope that some of those non-climbing squirrels might still be in sight. As they were not, he sighed unhappily and prepared to lay his classic young head back again on the rug for another spell of night-shortening sleep.

But, before his head could touch the rug, he reared it and half of his small body from the floor and focused his nearsighted eyes on the driveway. At the same time, his tail began to wag a thumping welcome.

Now, by day, a dog cannot see so far nor so clearly as can a human. But by night,—for comparatively short distances,—he can see much better than can his master. By day or by darkness, his keen hearing and keener scent make up for all defects of eyesight.

And now three of Lad's senses told him he was no longer alone in his tedious vigil. Down the drive, moving with amusing slowness and silence, a man was coming. He was on foot. And he was fairly well dressed. Dogs,—the foremost snobs in creation,—are quick to note the difference between a well-clad and a disreputable stranger.

Here unquestionably was a visitor:—some such man as so often came to the Place and paid such flattering attention to the puppy. No longer need Lad be bored by the solitude of this particular night. Some one was coming towards the house and carrying a small bag under his arm. Some one to make friends with. Lad was very happy.

Deep in his throat a welcoming bark was born. But he stilled it. Once, when he had barked at the approach of a stranger, the stranger had gone away. If this stranger were to go away, all the night's fun would go with him. Also, no later than yesterday, the Master had scolded Lad for barking at a man who had called. Wherefore the dog held his peace.

Getting to his feet and stretching himself, fore and aft, in true collie fashion, the pup gambolled up the drive to meet the visitor.

The man was feeling his way through the pitch darkness, groping cautiously; halting once or twice for a smoulder of lightning to silhouette the house he was nearing. In a wooded lane, a quarter mile away, his lightless motor car waited.

Lad trotted up to him, the tiny white feet noiseless in the soft dust of the drive. The man did not see him, but passed so close to the dog's hospitably upthrust nose that he all but touched it.

Only slightly rebuffed at such chill lack of cordiality, Lad fell in behind him, tail awag, and followed him to the porch. When the guest should ring the bell, the Master or one of the maids would come to the door. There would be lights and talk; and perhaps Laddie himself might be allowed to slip in to his beloved cave.

But the man did not ring. He did not stop at the door at all. On tiptoe he skirted the veranda to the old-fashioned bay windows at the south side of the living room;—windows with catches as old-fashioned and as simple to open as themselves.

Lad padded along, a pace or so to the rear;—still hopeful of being petted or perhaps even romped with. The man gave a faint but promising sign of intent to romp, by swinging his small and very shiny brown bag to and fro as he walked. Thus ever did the Master swing Lad's precious canton flannel doll before throwing it for him to retrieve. Lad made a tentative snap at the bag, his tail wagging harder than ever. But he missed it. And, in another moment the man stopped swinging the bag and tucked it under his arm again as he began to mumble with a bit of steel.

There was the very faintest of clicks. Then, noiselessly the window slid upward. A second fumbling sent the wooden inside shutters ajar. The man worked with no uncertainty. Ever since his visit to the Place, a week earlier, behind the ægis of a big and bright

33

and newly forged telephone-inspector badge, he had carried in his trained memory the location of windows and of obstructing furniture and of the primitive small safe in the living room wall, with its pitifully pickable lock;—the safe wherein the Place's few bits of valuable jewelry and other compact treasures reposed at night.

Lad was tempted to follow the creeping body and the fascinatingly swinging bag indoors. But his one effort to enter the house,—with muddy paws,—by way of an open window, had been rebuked by the Lawgivers. He had been led to understand that really well-bred little dogs come in by way of the door; and then only on permission.

So he waited, doubtfully, at the veranda edge; in the hope that his new friend might reappear or that the Master might perhaps want to show off his pup to the caller, as so often the Master was wont to do.

Head cocked to one side, tulip ears alert, Laddie stood listening. To the keenest human ears the thief's soft progress across the wide living room to the wall-safe would have been all but inaudible. But Lad could follow every phase of it;—the cautious skirting of each chair; the hesitant pause as a bit of ancient furniture creaked; the halt in front of the safe; the queer grinding noise, muffled but persevering, at the lock; then the faint creak of the swinging iron door, and the deft groping of fingers.

Soon, the man started back toward the paler oblong of gloom which marked the window's outlines from the surrounding black. Lad's tail began to wag again. Apparently, this eccentric person was coming out, after all, to keep him company. Now, the man was kneeling on the window-seat. Now, in gingerly fashion, he reached forward and set the small bag down on the veranda; before negotiating the climb across the broad seat,—a climb that might well call for the use of both his hands.

Lad was entranced. Here was a game he understood. Thus, more than once, had the Mistress tossed out to him his flannel doll, as he had stood in pathetic invitation on the porch, looking in at her as she read or talked. She had laughed at his wild tossings and other maltreatments of the limp doll. He had felt he was scoring a real hit. And this hit he decided to repeat.

Snatching up the swollen little satchel, almost before it left the intruder's hand, Lad shook it, joyously, revelling in the faint clink and jingle of the contents. He backed playfully away; the bag-handle swinging in his jaws. Crouching low, he wagged his tail in ardent invitation to the stranger to chase him and to get back the satchel. Thus did the Master romp with Lad when the flannel doll was the prize of their game. And Lad loved such races.

34

Yes, the stranger was accepting the invitation. The moment he had crawled out on the veranda he reached down for the bag. As it was not where he thought he had left it, he swung his groping hand forward in a half-circle, his fingers sweeping the floor.

Make that enticing motion, directly in front of a playful collie pup;—especially if he has something he doesn't want you to take from him;—and watch the effect.

Instantly, Lad was athrill with the spirit of the game. In one scurrying backward jump, he was off the veranda and on the lawn, tail vibrating, eyes dancing; satchel held tantalisingly towards its would-be possessor.

The light sound of his body touching ground reached the man. Reasoning that the sweep of his own arm had somehow knocked the bag off the porch, he ventured off the edge of the veranda and flashed a swathed ray of his pocket light along the ground in search of it.

The flashlight's lens was cleverly muffled; in a way to give forth but a single subdued finger of illumination. That one brief glimmer was enough to show the thief a right impossible sight. The glow struck answering lights from the polished sides of the brown bag. The bag was hanging in air some six inches above the grass and perhaps five feet away from him. Then he saw it swing frivolously to one side and vanish in the night.

The astonished man had seen more. Feeble was the flashlight's shrouded rag—too feeble to outline against the night the small dark body behind the shining brown bag. But that same ray caught and reflected back to the incredulous beholder two splashes of pale fire;—glints from a pair of deep-set collie-eyes.

As the bag disappeared, the eerie fire-points were gone. The thief all but dropped his flashlight. He gaped in nervous dread; and sought vainly to account for the witchwork he had witnessed.

He had plenty of nerve. He had plenty of experience along his chosen line of endeavour. But while a crook may control his nerve, he cannot make it phlegmatic or steady. Always, he must be conscious of holding it in check, as a clever driver checks and steadies and keeps in subjection a plunging horse. Let the vigilance slacken, and there is a runaway.

Now this particular marauder had long ago keyed his nerve to the chance of interruption from some gun-brandishing householder; and to the possible pursuit of police; and to the need of fighting or of fleeing. But all his preparations had not taken into account this newest emergency. He had not steeled himself to watch unmoved the gliding away of a treasure-satchel, apparently moving

35

of its own will; nor the shimmer of two greenish sparks in the air just above it. And, for an instant, the man had to battle against a craven desire to bolt.

Lad, meanwhile, was having a beautiful time. Sincerely, he appreciated the playful grab his nocturnal friend had made in his general direction. Lad had countered this, by frisking away for another five or six feet, and then wheeling about to face once more his playfellow and to await the next move in the blithe gambol. The pup could see tolerably well, in the darkness;—quite well enough to play the game his guest had devised. And of course, he had no way of knowing that the man could not see equally well.

Shaking off his momentary terror, the thief once more pressed the button of his flashlight; swinging the torch in a swift semicircle and extinguishing it at once; lest the dim glow be seen by any wakeful member of the family.

That one quick sweep revealed to his gaze the shiny brown bag a half-dozen feet ahead of him, still swinging several inches above ground. He flung himself forward at it; refusing to believe he also saw that queer double glow of pale light, just above. He dived for the satchel with the speed and the accuracy of a football tackle. And that was all the good it did him.

Perhaps there is something in nature more agile and dismayingly elusive than a romping young collie. But that "something" is not a mortal man. As the thief sprang, Lad sprang in unison with him; darting to the left and a yard or so backward. He came to an expectant standstill once more; his tail wildly vibrating, his entire furry body tingling with the glad excitement of the game. This Sportive visitor of his was a veritable godsend. If only he could be coaxed into coming to play with him every night—!

But presently he noted that the other seemed to have wearied of the game. After plunging through the air and landing on all fours with his grasping hands closing on nothingness, the man had remained thus, as if dazed, for a second or so. Then he had felt the ground all about him. Then, bewildered, he had scrambled to his feet. Now he was standing, moveless, his lips working.

Yes, he seemed to be tired of the lovely game—and just when Laddie was beginning to enter into the full spirit of it. Once in a while, the Mistress or the Master stopped playing, during the romps with the flannel doll. And Laddie had long since hit on a trick for reviving their interest. He employed this ruse now.

As the man stood, puzzled and scared, something brushed very lightly,—even coquettishly,—against his knuckles. He started in nervous fright. An instant later, the same thing brushed his

36

knuckles again, this time more insistently. The man, in a spurt of fear-driven rage, grabbed at the invisible object. His fingers slipped along the smooth sides of the bewitched bag that Lad was shoving invitingly at him.

Brief as was the contact, it was long enough for the thief's sensitive finger tips to recognise what they touched. And both hands were brought suddenly into play, in a mad snatch for the prize. The ten avid fingers missed the bag; and came together with clawing force. But, before they met, the finger tips of the left hand telegraphed to the man's brain that they had had momentary light experience with something hairy and warm—something that had slipped, eel-like, past them into the night;—something that most assuredly was no satchel, but alive!

The man's throat contracted, in gagging fright. And, as before, fear scourged him to feverish rage.

Recklessly he pressed the flashlight's button; and swung the muffled bar of light in every direction. In his other hand he levelled the pistol he had drawn. This time the shaded ray revealed to him not only his bag, but,—vaguely,—the Thing that held it.

He could not make out what manner of creature it was which gripped the satchel's handle and whose eyes pulsed back greenish flares into the torch's dim glow. But it was an animal of some kind;—distorted and formless in the wavering finger of blunted light, but still an animal. Not a ghost.

And fear departed. The intruder feared nothing mortal. The mystery in part explained, he did not bother to puzzle out the remainder of it. Impossible as it seemed, his bag was carried by some living thing. All that remained for him was to capture the thing, and recover his bag. The weak light still turned on, he gave chase.

Lad's spirits arose with a bound. His ruse had succeeded. He had reawakened in this easily-discouraged chum a new interest in the game. And he gambolled across the lawn, fairly wriggling with delight. He did not wish to make his friend lose interest again. So instead of dashing off at full speed, he frisked daintily, just out of reach of the clawing hand.

And in this pleasant fashion the two playfellows covered a hundred yards of ground. More than once, the man came within an inch of his quarry. But always, by the most imperceptible spurt of speed, Laddie arranged to keep himself and his dear satchel from capture.

Then, in no time at all, the game ended; and with it ended Lad's baby faith in the friendliness and trustworthiness of all human nature.

37

Realising that the sound of his own stumbling running feet and the intermittent flashes of his torch might well awaken some light sleeper in the house, the thief resolved on a daring move. This creature in front of him,—dog or bear or goat, or whatever it was,—was uncatchable. But by sending a bullet through it, he could bring the animal to a sudden and permanent stop.

Then, snatching up his bag and running at top speed, he himself could easily win clear of the Place before any one of the household should appear. And his car would be a mile away before the neighbourhood could be aroused. Fury at the weird beast and the wrenching strain on his own nerves lent eagerness to his acceptance of the idea.

He reached back again for his pistol, whipped it out, and, coming to a standstill, aimed at the pup. Lad, waiting only to bound over an obstruction in his path, came to a corresponding pause, not ten feet ahead of his playmate.

It was an easy shot. Yet the bullet went several inches above the obligingly waiting dog's back. Nine men out of ten, shooting by moonlight or by flashlight, aim too high. The thief had heard this old marksman-maxim fifty times. But, like most hearers of maxims, he had forgotten it at the one time in his speckled career when it might have been of any use to him.

He had fired. He had missed. In another second, every sleeper in the house and in the gate-lodge would be out of bed. His night's work was a blank, unless—

With a bull rush he hurled himself forward at the interestedly waiting Lad. And, as he sprang, he fired again. Then several things happened.

Every one, except movie actors and newly-appointed policemen, knows that a man on foot cannot shoot straight, unless he is standing stock still. Yet, as luck would have it, this second shot found a mark where the first and better aimed bullet had gone wild.

Lad had leaped the narrow and deep ditch left along the lawn-edge by workers who were putting in a new water-main for the Place. On the far side of this obstacle he had stopped, and had waited for his friend to follow. But the friend had not followed. Instead, he had been somehow responsible for a spurt of red flame and for a most thrilling racket. Lad was more impressed than ever by the man's wondrous possibilities as a midnight entertainer. He waited, gaily expectant, for more. He got it.

There was a second rackety explosion and a second puff of lightning from the man's outflung hand. But, this time, something like a red-hot whip-lash smote Lad with horribly agonising force athwart the right hip.

38

The man had done this,—the man whom Laddie had thought so friendly and playful!

He had not done it by accident. For his hand had been outflung directly at the pup, just as once had been the arm of the kennelman, back at Lad's birthplace, in beating a disobedient mongrel. It was the only beating Lad had ever seen. And it had stuck, shudderingly, in his uncannily sensitive memory. Yet now, he himself had just had a like experience.

In an instant, the pup's trustful friendliness was gone. The man had come on the Place, at dead of night, and had struck him. That must be paid for! Never would the pup forget his agonising lesson that night intruders are not to be trusted or even to be tolerated. Within a single second, he had graduated from a little friend of all the world, into a vigilant watchdog.

With a snarl, he dropped the bag and whizzed forward at his assailant. Needle-sharp milkteeth bared, head low, ruff abristle, friendly soft eyes as ferocious as a wolf's, he charged.

There had been scarce a breathing-space between the second report of the pistol and the collie's counter-attack. But there had been time enough for the onward-plunging thief to step into the narrow lip of the water-pipe ditch. The momentum of his own rush hurled the upper part of his body forward. But his left leg, caught between the ditch-sides, did not keep pace with the rest of him. There was a hideous snapping sound, a screech of mortal anguish; and the man crashed to earth, in a dead faint of pain and shock,— his broken left leg still thrust at an impossible angle in the ditch.

Lad checked himself midway in his own fierce charge. Teeth bare, throat agrowl, he hesitated. It had seemed to him right and natural to assail the man who had struck him so painfully. But now this same man was lying still and helpless under him. And the sporting instincts of a hundred generations of thoroughbreds cried out to him not to mangle the defenceless.

Wherefore, he stood, irresolute; alert for sign of movement on the part of his foe. But there was no such sign. And the light bullet-graze on his hip was hurting like the very mischief.

Moreover, every window in the house beyond was blossoming forth into lights. There were sounds,—reassuring human sounds. And doors were opening. His deities were coming forth.

All at once, Laddie stopped being a vengeful beast of prey; and remembered that he was a very small and very much hurt and very lonely and worried puppy. He craved the Mistress's dear touch on his wound, and a word of crooning comfort from her soft voice. This yearning was mingled with a doubt less perhaps he had been

39

transgressing the Place's Law, in some new way; and lest he might have let himself in for a scolding. The Law was still so queer and so illogical!

Lad started toward the house. Then, pausing, he picked up the bag which had been so exhilarating a plaything for him this past few minutes and which he had forgotten in his pain.

It was Lad's collie way to pick up offerings (ranging from slippers to very dead fish) and to carry them to the Mistress. Sometimes he was petted for this. Sometimes the offering was lifted gingerly between aloof fingers and tossed back into the lake. But, nobody could well refuse so jingly and pretty a gift as this satchel.

The Master, sketchily attired, came running down the lawn, flashlight in hand. Past him, unnoticed, as he sped toward the ditch, a collie pup limped;—a very unhappy and comfort-seeking puppy who carried in his mouth a blood-spattered brown bag.

"It doesn't make sense to me!" complained the Master, next day, as he told the story for the dozenth time, to a new group of callers. "I heard the shots and I went out to investigate. There he was lying half in and half out of the ditch. The fellow was unconscious. He didn't get his senses back till after the police came. Then he told some babbling yarn about a creature that had stolen his bag of loot and that had lured him to the ditch. He was all unnerved and upset, and almost out of his head with pain. So the police had little enough trouble in 'sweating' him. He told everything he knew. And there's a wholesale round-up of the motor-robbery bunch going on this afternoon as a result of it. But what I can't understand—"

"It's as clear as day," insisted the Mistress, stroking a silken head that pressed lovingly against her knee. "As clear as day. I was standing in the doorway here when Laddie came pattering up to me and laid a little satchel at my feet. I opened it, and—well, it had everything of value in it that had been in the safe over there. That and the thief's story make it perfectly plain. Laddie caught the man as he was climbing out of that window. He got the bag away from him; and the man chased him, firing as he went. And he stumbled into the ditch and—"

"Nonsense!" laughed the Master. "I'll grant all you say about Lad's being the most marvellous puppy on earth. And I'll even believe all the miracles of his cleverness. But when it comes to taking a bag of jewelry from a burglar and then enticing him to a ditch and then coming back here to you with the bag—"

"Then how do you account—?"

"I don't. None of it makes sense to me. As I just said. But,—

40

whatever happened, it's turned Laddie into a real watchdog. Did you notice how he went for the police when they started down the drive, last night? We've got a watchdog at last."

"We've got more than a watchdog," amended the Mistress. "An ordinary watchdog would just scare away thieves or bite them. Lad captured the thief and then brought the stolen jewelry back to us. No other dog could have done that."

Lad, enraptured by the note of praise in the Mistress's soft voice, looked adoringly up into the face that smiled so proudly down at him. Then, catching the sound of a step on the drive, he dashed out to bark in murderous fashion at a wholly harmless delivery boy whom he had seen every day for weeks.

A watchdog can't afford to relax vigilance, for a single instant,—especially at the responsible age of five months.

THREE

The Meanest Man

The big collie lay at ease, his tawny-and-white length stretched out in lazy luxury across the mouth of the lane which led from the Hampton highroad to Link Ferris' hillside farmhouse.

Of old, this lane had been rutted and grass-hummocked and bordered by tangles of rusty weeds. Since Link and his farm had taken so decided a brace, the weeds had been cut away. This without even a hint from the county engineer, who of old had so often threatened to fine Link for leaving them standing along the highway at his land's edge. The lane had been graded and ditched, too, into a neatness that went well with the rest of the place.

But—now that Link Ferris had taken to himself a wife, as efficient as she was pretty—it had been decreed by young Mrs. Ferris that the lane's entrance should be enhanced still further by the erecting of two low fieldstone piers, one on either side, and that the hollow at the top of each pier should be filled with loam for the planting of nasturtiums.

It was on this decorative job that Link was at work to-day. His collie, Chum, was always near at hand wherever his master chanced to be toiling. And Chum, now, was lying comfortably on the soft earth of the lane head, some fifty feet from where Link wrought with rock and mortar.

Up the highroad, from Hampton village a mile below, jogged a bony yellow horse, drawing a ramshackle vehicle which looked like the ghost of a delivery wagon. The wagon had a sharp tilt to one side. For long years it had been guiltless of paint. Its canvas sides were torn and stained. Its rear was closed by a wabbly grating. The axles and whiffletree emitted a combination of grievously complaining squeaks from the lack of grease. And other and still more grievous noises issued from the grated recesses of the cart.

On the sagging seat sprawled a beefy man whose pendulous cheeks seemed the vaster for the narrowness of his little eyes. These eyes were wandering inquiringly from side to side along Link's land boundary, until they chanced to light upon the recumbent collie. Then into their shallow recesses glinted a look of sharp interest. It was on this collie's account that the man had driven out from Hampton to-day. His drive was a reconnoitre.

He clucked his bony steed to a faster jog, his gaze fixed with growing avidity on the dog. As he neared the mouth of the lane, he caught sight of Link and the narrow orbs lost a shade of their jubilance.

So might a pedestrian's eyes have glinted at sight of a dollar bill on the sidewalk in front of him. So might the glint have clouded on seeing the bill's owner reaching down for his property. The simile is not far-fetched, for the driver, on viewing Chum, had fancied he beheld the equivalent of several dollars.

He was Eben Shunk, official poundmaster and dog catcher of Hampton Borough. Each and every stray dog caught and impounded by him meant the sum of one dollar to be paid him, in due form, by the Hampton Borough treasurer. And the fact that Chum's sturdy master was within hail of the invitingly supine collie vexed the thrifty soul of Eben Shunk.

Yet there was hope. And upon this hope Eben staked his chances for the elusive dollar and for the main object of his visit—which was no mere dollar. Briefly, in his mind, he reviewed the case and the possibilities and laid out his plan of campaign. Halting his bony horse at the mouth of the lane, he hailed Link.

"Look-a-here!" he called. "Did you take out a license for that big mutt of your'n yet?"

Link glanced up from his work, viewed the visitor with no semblance of favour and made curt reply.

"I didn't. And he ain't."

"Huh?" queried Mr. Shunk, puzzled at this form of answer.

"I didn't license him," expounded Link, "and he ain't a mutt. If that's all you've stopped your trav'lin' m'nagerie at my lane for, you can move it on as quick as you're a mind to."

He bent over his work again. But Eben Shunk did not take the hint.

"'Cordin' to the laws an' statoots of the Borough of Hampton, county of P'saic, state of Noo Jersey," proclaimed the dog catcher with much dignity, "it's my perk's't an' dooty to impound each an' every unlicensed dog found in the borough limits."

"Well," assented Link, "go on and impound 'em, then. Only don't pester me about it. I'm not int'rested. S'pose you get that old bag of bones to haul your rattletrap junk cart somewheres else! I'm busy."

"Bein' a smarty won't get you nowheres!" declared Shunk. "If your dog ain't licensed, it's my dooty to impound him. He—"

"Here!" snapped Link. "You got your answer on that when you tackled my wife about it down to her father's store last week. She

43

told me all about it. You came a-blusterin' in there while she was buyin' some goods and while Chum was standin' peaceful beside her. You said if he wasn't licensed he'd be put in pound. And if it hadn't been for her dad and the clerk throwin' you out of the store, you'd 'a' grabbed him, then and there. She told you, then, that we pay the state and county tax on the dog and that the law doesn't compel us to pay any other tax or any license fee for him. If your borough council wanted to get some easy graft by passing an ordinance for ev'ry res'dent of Hampton Borough to pay one dollar a year license fees on their dogs—well, that's their business. It's not mine. My home's not in the borough and—"

"Some says it is an' some says it ain't," interrupted Shunk. "The south bound'ry of the borough was shifted, by law, last month. An' the line takes in more'n a half-acre of your south woodlot. So you're a res'd'nt of—"

"I don't live in my south woodlot," contradicted Link, "nor yet within half a mile of it. I—"

"That's for the courts to d'cide," said Shunk. "Pers'n'lly, I hold you're a borough res'd'nt. An' since you ain't paid your fee, your dog is forf't to—"

"I see!" put in Ferris. "You'll grab the dog and you'll get your dirty dollar fee from the borough treasury. Then if the law decides my home is out of the borough, you'll still have your money. You're a clever man, Shunk."

"Well," averred the dog catcher, mildly pleased with the compliment, "it ain't for me to say as to that. But there don't many folks find me a-nappin', I'm sittin' here to tell all an' sundry. Now, 'bout that dog—"

"Yes," repeated Link admiringly, "you're a mighty clever man! Only I've figgered that you aren't quite clever enough to spell your own name right. Folks who know you real well think you've got an 'h' in it that ought to be a 'k.' But that's no fault of yours, Shunk. You do your best to live up to the name you ought by rights to have. So"

"You'll leave my name be!" thundered the dog catcher.

"I sure will," assented Link. "By the way, did you ever happen to hear how near you came to not gettin' this office of dog catcher down at Hampton?"

"No," grunted the other, "I didn't hear nothin' of the kind. An' it ain't true. Mayor Wipple app'inted me, same week as he took office—like he had promised he would if I'd git my brother an' the three boys to vote for him an' if I'd c'ntribbit thutty-five dollars to his campaign fund. There wasn't ever any doubt I'd git the app'intment."

44

"Oh, yes, there was," cheerily denied Link, with a sidelong glance at his pretty wife and her six-year-old sister, Olive Chatham, who were advancing along the lane from the house to note the progress of the stonework piers. "There was a lot of doubt. If it hadn't been for just one thing you'd never have landed the job.

"It was this way," he continued, winking encouragement to Mrs. Ferris who had come to a momentary and disapproving halt at sight of her husband's uninvited guest. "The day after Wipple was elected mayor, I asked him who he was aiming to appoint to the high and loocrative office of dog catcher. He told me he was goin' to appoint you. I says to him, 'But Eben Shunk's the meanest man in town!' And Wipple answers 'I know he is. He's as mean as pussly. That's why I've picked him out for dog catcher. No decent feller would take such a dirty job.' That's what Mayor Wipple told me, Shunk. So you see if you hadn't happened to be the meanest man in Hampton, you'd never 'a' got—"

"It's a durn lie!" bellowed the irate Shunk. "It's a lie! Wipple never said no such a thing. He—"

"What's in the wagon, there?" spoke up little Olive Chatham, as a dolorous whimpering rose from the depths of the covered cart. "It sounds awful unhappy."

"It is 'awful unhappy,' Baby," answered her brother-in-law. "Mr. Shunk has been on his rounds, picking up some more poor little stray curs, along the road. He's going to carry them to a filthy pen in his filthy back yard and leave them to starve and be chewed by bigger dogs there, while he pikes off to get his dollar, each, for them. Then, if they aren't claimed and licensed in twenty-four hours, he's going to—"

"Link!" interposed Dorcas, his wife, warningly, as she visualised the effect of such a word picture on her little sister's tender heart.

But Olive had heard enough to set her baby eyes ablaze with indignation. Wheeling on Link, she demanded:

"Why don't you whip him and let out all those poor little dogs? And then why don't you go and put him in prison for—"

"Hush, dear!" whispered Dorcas, drawing the little girl close to her. "Better run back to the house now! That isn't a nice sort of man for you to be near."

Eben Shunk caught the low-spoken words. They served to snap the last remaining threads of the baited dog catcher's temper. His fists clenched and he took a step toward Ferris. But the latter's lazily wiry figure did not seem to lend itself to the idea of passivity under punishment. Shunk's angry little eyes fell on the collie.

45

"That dog of your'n ain't licensed," he said. "He's layin' out on the public road. An' I'm goin' to take him along."

"Go ahead," vouchsafed Link indifferently, with a covert glance of reassurance at his scandalised wife, who had made a family idol of Chum. "He's there. Nobody's stoppin' you."

Pleased at meeting with no stouter resistance from the owner, Shunk took a step toward the recumbent collie. Little Olive cried out in hot protest. Link bent over her and whispered in her ear. The child's face lost its look of panic and shone with pleased interest as she watched Eben bear down upon his victim. Ferris whistled hissingly between his teeth—an intermittent staccato blast. Then he, too, turned an interested gaze on the impending capture.

Chum had not enjoyed the past few minutes at all. His loafing inspection of his master's job had been interrupted by the arrival of this loud-voiced stranger. He did not like the stranger. Chum decided that, at his first glimpse and scent of the man—and the dog catcher's voice had confirmed the distaste. Shunk belonged to the type which sensitive dogs hate instinctively. But Chum was too well versed in the guest law to molest or snarl at any one with whom Link was in seemingly amicable talk. So he had paid no overt heed to the fellow.

There were other and more interesting things, moreover, which had caught Chum's attention. The sounds and scents from the wagon's unseen interior carried to him a message of fear, of pain, of keen sorrow. Chum had half-risen, to investigate. Link, noting the action, had signalled the dog to lie down again. And Chum, as always, had obeyed.

But now, through his sullen brooding, pierced a sound that set every one of the collie's lively nerves aquiver. It was a hissing whistle—broken and staccato. It was a signal Link had made up, years ago—a signal which always brought the dog to him on the gallop. For that signal meant no summons to a romp. It spelled mischief. For example, when cattle chanced to stroll in from the highway, that whistle signified leave for the dog to run them, pell-mell, down the road, with barks and nips—instead of driving them decorously and slowly, as he drove his own master's cows. It had a similar message when tramp or mongrel invaded the farm.

At the sound of it, now, Chum was on his feet in an instant. He found himself confronting the obnoxious stranger, who was just reaching forward to clutch him.

Chum eluded the man and started toward Link. Shunk made a wild grab for him. Chum's ruff—a big handful of it—was seized in the clutching fingers. Again sounded that queer whistle. This time—

thanks to the years of close companionship between dog and master—Chum caught its purport. Evidently, it had something to do with Shunk, with the man who had laid hold on him so unceremoniously.

Chum glanced quickly at Link. Ferris was grinning. With an imperceptible nod of the head he indicated Shunk. The dog understood. At least, he understood enough for his own purposes. The law was off of this disgusting outlander. Ferris was trying to enlist the collie's aid in harrying him. It was a right welcome task.

In a flash, Chum had twisted his silken head. A single slash of his white eyetooth had laid open the fat wrist of the fat hand that gripped him. Shunk, with a yell, loosed his hold and jumped back. He caught the echo of a smothered chuckle from Link and turned to find the Ferrises and the child surveying the scene with happy excitement—looking for all the world like three people at an amusing picture show. The dog catcher bolted for his wagon and plunged the lacerated arm into the box beneath the seat. Thence he drew it forth, clutching in his hand a coil of noosed rope and a strong oversized landing net.

"Tools of his trade!" explained Link airily, to his wife and Olive.

As he spoke, Ferris made a motion of his forefinger toward the tensely expectant dog and thence toward the lane. The gesture was familiar from sheep herding experience. At once, Chum darted back a few yards and stood just inside the boundaries of his master's land. A clucking sound from Link told him where to halt. And the collie stood there, tulip ears cocked, plumy tail awag, eyes abrim with mischief, as he waited his adversary's next move. Seldom did Chum have so appreciative an audience to show off before.

Shunk, rope and net in hand, bore down upon his prey. As he came on he cleared decks for action by yanking his coat off and slinging it across one shoulder. Thus his arms would work unimpeded. So eagerly did he advance to the hunt that he paid no heed to Link. Wherefore, he failed to note a series of unobtrusive gestures and clucks and nods with which Link guided his furtively observing dog.

The next two minutes were of interest. Shunk unslung his rope as he advanced. Five feet away from the politely waiting collie he paused and flung the noose. He threw with practised skill. The wide noose encircled the dog. But before Shunk could tighten it, Chum had sprung lightly out of the contracting circle and, at a move of Link's finger, had backed a few feet farther onto Ferris's own property.

47

Chagrined at his miss and spurred on by the triple chuckle of his audience, the man coiled his rope and flung it a second time. Temper and haste spoiled his aim. He missed the dog clean. Baby Olive laughed aloud. Chum fairly radiated contempt at such poor marksmanship. Coiling his rope as, at another signal, Chum backed a little farther away, Shunk shouted:

"I'll git ye, yet! An' when I do, I'll tie you to a post in my yard an' muzzle you. Then I'll take a club to you, till there ain't a whole bone left in yer carcass. If Ferris buys you free, there won't be more'n sassage-meat fer him to tote home."

Olive gasped. The grin left Link's face. Dorcas looked up appealingly at her husband. Shunk flung his noose a third time. Chum, well understanding now what was expected of him, bounded far backward.

"Get off of my land!" called Ferris, in a queerly gentle and almost humble voice.

"When I take this cur off'n it with me!" snarled the catcher, too hot on the quest to be wholly sane.

He coiled his rope once more. At a gesture from Link, the dog lay down.

"In the presence of a competent witness I've ordered you off my land," repeated Ferris, in that same meek voice. "You've refused. The law allows me to use force in such a case. It—"

Deceived by the humility of the tone and lured by the dog's new passivity, Shunk made one final cast of the noose. This time its folds settled round the collie's massive throat ruff. In the same fraction of a second, Ferris yelled:

"Take him, Chum! Take him!"

The dog heard and most gleefully he obeyed. As the triumphant Shunk drew tight the noose about his victim's neck and sought to bring the landing net into play, Chum launched himself, like a furry catapult, full at the man's throat.

And now there was no hint of fun or of mischief in the collie's deep-set dark eyes. They flamed into swirling fury. He had received the word to attack. And he obeyed with a fiery zest. So may Joffre's grim legions have felt, in 1914, when, at the Marne, they were told they need no longer keep up the hated retreat, but might turn upon their German foes and pay the bill for the past months' humiliations.

As the furious collie sprang, Shunk instinctively sought to clap the landing net's thick meshes over Chum's head. But the dog was too swift for him. The wooden side of the net smote, almost unfelt, against the fur-protected skull. The impact sent it flying out of its wielder's grasp.

48

The blow checked the collie's charge by the barest instant. And in that instant, Shunk wheeled and fled. Just behind him was a shellbark tree, with a low limb jutting out above the lane. Shunk dropped his coat and leaped for this overhanging limb as Chum made a second dash for him.

The man's fingers closed round the branch and he sought to draw himself up, screaming loudly for help. The scream redoubled in volume and scaled half an octave in pitch as the pursuing collie's teeth met in Shunk's calf.

His flabby muscles galvanised by pain and by terror, the man made shift to drag his weight upward and to fling a leg over the branch. But as the right leg hooked itself across the bough, the dangling left leg felt a second embrace from the searing white teeth, in a slashing bite that clove through trouser and sock and skin and flesh and grated against the bone itself.

Screeching and mouthing, Shunk wriggled himself up onto the branch and lay hugging it with both arms and both punctured legs. Below him danced and snarled Chum, launching himself high in air, again and again, in a mad effort to get at his escaped prey. Then the dog turned to the approaching Ferris in stark appeal for help in dislodging the intruder from his precarious perch.

"That's enough, Chummie!" drawled Link. "Leave him be!"

He petted the dog's head and smiled amusedly at Chum's visible reluctance in abandoning the delightful game of man treeing. At a motion of Ferris's hand, the collie walked reluctantly away and lay down beside Dorcas.

Chum could never understand why humans had such a habit of calling him off—just when fun was at its height. It was like this when he ran stray cattle off the farm or chased predatory tramps. Still, Link was his god; obedience was Chum's creed. Wherefore, so far as he was concerned, Eben Shunk ceased to exist.

The dog catcher noted the cessation of attack. And he ceased his own howls. He drew himself to a painful sitting posture on the tree limb and began to nurse one of his torn legs.

"You'll go to jail for this!" he whined down at Ferris.

"I'll swear out a warr'nt agin ye, the minute I git back to Hampton. Yes, an' I'll git the judge to order your dog shot as a men'ce to public safety an'—"

"I guess not!" Ferris cut him short as Shunk's whine swelled to a howl. "I guess not, Mister Meanest Man. In fact, you'll be lucky if you keep out of the hoosgow, on my charge of trespass. You came onto my land against my wish. You couldn't help seein' my No Trespassing sign yonder. I ordered you off. You refused to go. I gave

49

you fair warnin'. You wouldn't mind it. I did all that before I sicked the dog on you. My wife is a reli'ble witness. And she can swear to it in any court. If I sick my dog onto a trespasser who refuses to clear out when he's told to, there's no law in North Jersey that will touch either me or Chum. And you know it as well as I do. Now I tell you once more to clear off of my farm. If you'll go quick I'll see the dog don't bother you. If you put up any more talk I'll station him under this tree and leave you and him to companion each other here all day. Now git!"

As though to impress his presence once more on Mr. Shunk, Chum slowly got up from the ground at Dorcas' feet and slouched lazily toward the tree again. Link, wondering at the dog's apparent disobedience of his command to leave the prisoner alone, looked on with a frown of perplexity. But at once his face cleared.

For Chum was not honouring the tree dweller by so much as a single upward glance. Instead, he was picking his way to where Shunk's discarded coat lay on the ground near the tree foot. The dog stood over this unlovely garment, looking down at its greasily worn surface with sniffling disapproval. Then, with much cold deliberation, Chum knelt down and thrust one of his great furry shoulders against the rumpled surface of the coat and shoved the shoulder along the unkempt expanse of cloth. After which he repeated the same performance with his other shoulder, ending the demonstration by rolling solemnly and luxuriously upon the rumpled, mishandled coat.

Link burst into a bellow of Homeric laughter. Shunk, peering down, went purple with utter and speechless indignation. Both men understood dogs. Therefore, to both of them, Chum's purpose was as clear as day. But Baby Olive looked on in crass perplexity. She wondered why Link found it so funny.

"What's he doing, Link?" she demanded. "What's Chummie rolling on that nassy ol' coat for? It'll get him all dirty."

"Listen, Baby," exhorted Link, when he could speak. "A dog never digs his shoulders into anything, that way, and then rolls in it—except carrion! He—"

"Link!" cried Dorcas, scandalised.

"That's so, old girl," replied her husband. "It's a busy day and we won't have time to waste in giving the dog a bath. Come away, Chum!"

The dog came back to his place in front of Dorcas. Ferris, wearying of the scene, nodded imperatively to Shunk.

"Come down!" he decreed. "It's safe. So long as you get out of here, now!"

Mouthing, gobbling like some distressed turkey, Eben Shunk proceeded to let his bulk down from the limb. He groaned in active misery as his bitten legs were called upon to bear his weight again. He stood for a moment glowering from Link to the disgruntedly passive collie. Chum returned the look with compound interest, then glanced at Ferris in wistful appeal, dumbly begging leave to renew the chase.

Shunk still fought for coherent utterance and weighed in his bemused brain the fact that he had overstepped the law. Before he could speak, a pleasant diversion was caused by Olive Chatham.

The little girl had been a happily interested spectator of the bout between her adored Chum and this pig-eyed fat man. But the coat-rolling episode had been beyond her comprehension. She had trotted away, after Link's explanation of it, and her mind had cast about for some new excitement. She had found it.

The bony yellow horse had been left untied; in Shunk's haste to annex a dog-catching dollar. Therefore the horse, after the manner of his kind, had begun to crop the wayside grass. But this grass was close cut and was hard for his decaying teeth to nibble. A little farther on, just within the limits of the lane, the herbage grew lusher and higher. So the horse had strayed thither, trundling his disreputable wagon after him.

Olive's questing glance had fallen upon horse and cart, not ten feet away from her, and several yards inside of the farm's boundary line. She heard also that pitiful sound of whimpering from within the canvas-covered body of the wagon. And she remembered what Link had said about the dogs imprisoned there.

She hurried up to the vehicle and circumnavigated it until she came to the grating at the back.

Clambering up on the rear step, she looked in. At once several pathetically sniffing little noses were thrust through the bars for a caress or a kind word in that abode of loneliness and fear.

This was too much for the child's warm heart. She resolved then and there upon the rôle of deliverer. Reaching up to the grated door, she pushed back its simple bolt.

Instantly she was half-buried under a canine avalanche. No fewer than seven dogs—all small and all badly scared—bounded through the open doorway toward freedom. In their dash for safety they almost knocked the baby to the ground. Then with joyous barks and yelps they galloped off in every direction.

This was the spectacle which smote upon the horrified senses of Eben Shunk as he fought for words under the tree that had been his abode of refuge.

Shunk had had an unusually profitable morning. Not often did a single day's work net him seven dollars. But this was circus day at Paterson and many Hampton people had gone thither. They had left their dogs at home. One or two of these dogs had wandered onto the street, where they had fallen easy victims to the dog catcher. Others he had snatched, protesting, from the porches and dooryards of their absent owners. Seven of the lot had not chanced to wear license tags, and these Shunk had corralled in his wagon. Now his best day's work in months threatened to become a total loss.

With a wild wrench he drove his arms into the sleeves of the coat he had just rescued. In the same series of motions—and bawling an assortment of expletives, which Link hoped Dorcas and Olive might not understand—the dog catcher made a wild rush for his escaped captives, picking up and brandishing the landing net as he ran.

"Chum!" whispered Ferris tensely.

As he spoke he pointed to the bony yellow horse.

"Easy!" he added, observing the steed's feebleness and age.

The yellow horse was roused from his first square meal in weeks by a gentle nip at his heel. He threw up his head with a snort and made a clumsy bound forward.

But, instantly, Chum was in front of him, herding him as often he had herded recalcitrant cows of Link's, steering him for the highroad. As the wagon creaked and bumped out onto the turnpike, Chum imparted a farewell nip to one of the charger's hocks.

With a really creditable burst of speed the horse set off down the road at a hand gallop. The rattle and squeaking of the disreputable wagon reached Shunk's ears just as Eben had almost cornered one of the seven escaping dogs.

Shunk turned round. Down the road his horse was running. A sharp turn was barely quarter of a mile beyond. On the stone of this turn the brute might well shatter the wagon and perhaps injure himself. There was but one thing for his distracted owner to do. Horse and wagon were worth more than seven dollars—even if not very much more. Eben Shunk was a thrifty man. And he knew he must forgo the capture of the seven rescued dogs if he intended to save his equipage.

He broke into a run, giving chase to his faithless steed. As he passed the thunderously guffawing Ferris, Shunk wasted enough precious breath and time to yell:

"I'll git that dog of yourn yet! Next time he sets foot in Hampton Borough I'll—"

The rest of his threat was lost in distance.

"H'm!" mused Ferris, the laugh dying on his lips. "He'll do it too! He'll be layin' in wait for Chum, if it takes a year. In the borough limits dogs and folks is bound by borough laws. That means we can't take Chum to Hampton again. Unless—Lord, but folks can stir up more ructions over a decent innocent dog than over all the politics that ever happened! If—"

His maundering voice trailed away. Just before him, at the spot where Shunk had jettisoned his defiled and much-rolled-on coat, was a scrap of paper. It was dirty and it was greasy and it had been folded in a half sheet. His hard-learned lessons in neatness impelled Link to stoop and pick up this bit of litter which marred the clean surface of the sward. The doubled half sheet opened in his hand as he glanced carelessly at it. The first of several sentences scrawled thereon leaped forth to meet the man's gaze.

Ferris stuck the paper in his shirt pocket and stared down the road after the receding Shunk with a smoulder in his eye that might have stirred that village functionary to some slight alarm had he seen it.

Olive's visit to her big sister ended a week later. Link and Dorcas escorted her back to the Chathams' Hampton home. Old Man Chatham ran the village's general store and post office and had the further distinction of being a local justice of the peace.

Olive did not at all care for the idea of changing her outdoor life at the Ferris farm for a return to the metropolitan roar and jostle of a village with nine hundred inhabitants. And she showed her disapproval by sitting in solemn and semi-tearful silence on the slippery back seat of Link's ancient carryall all the short way into town. Only as the carryall was drawing up in front of the store, which occupied the southerly half of her ancestral home, did she break silence. Then she said aggrievedly:

"This is just like when I get punished. And poor Chummie got punished, too, for something. Why did Chummie get punished, Link?"

"Old Chum never got punished in his life," answered Link. "Whatever gave you that notion, Baby?"

"When I looked for him, to say by-by," explained Olive, "he wasn't anywheres at all. So I called at him. And he barked. And I went to where the bark was. And there was poor old Chummie all tied up to a chain in the barn. He was being punished. So I—"

"He wasn't being punished, dear," said Dorcas, lifting the child to the ground. "Link tied him up so he wouldn't follow us to town. There are so many autos on the roads Saturday afternoons. Besides, Eben Shunk—"

53

"Oh," queried Olive. "Was that why? I thought he was punished. So I unpunished him. I let him loose. Not outdoors. Because maybe you'd see him and tie him again. I let him loose and I shut the barn door, so he could stay in there and play and not be tied."

"It'd take Chum just about ten minutes to worry the barn door open!" grinned Link. "He'll get our scent and come pirootin' straight after us."

"Oh!" exclaimed Dorcas. "Hadn't you better turn back and—"

But the hurrying of the child's father and mother from the house to welcome the newcomers drove the thought out of her mind. Link had but grinned the wider at her troubled suggestion. Greeting his parents-in-law, Ferris hitched his horse and followed Dorcas and her mother to the veranda.

There they sat talking until suddenly a volley of heart-broken screams broke in upon them. Up the path from the street rushed little Olive, her eyes streaming, her baby mouth in a wide circle, from which issued a series of panic cries.

Both men sprang to their feet and hurried down the path to meet her. Her mother and sister rushed from the house at the same moment and ran to succour the screaming child. But Olive thrust them back, squealing frantically to Link:

"That awful man's got Chummie! He tooked him from me and he says he'll beat him till he's dead. I pulled Chummie away and the man slapped me over and he's running off with Chummie!"

Old Man Chatham was an elder in the church at Hampton. Yet on hearing of the blow administered to his worshipped child and at the sight of an ugly red mark athwart her plump baby face, an expletive crackled luridly from between his pious lips—an expletive which should have brought him before the consistory of his church for rigid discipline.

Then, by the time Olive had sobbed out her pitiful tidings, both he and Link Ferris had set off down the street at a dead run. Instinctively they were heading for an alley which bisected the street a furlong below—an alley wherein abode Eben Shunk and where his backyard pound was maintained.

Truly, Chum had let himself and others in for an abundance of trouble when he scratched and nosed at the recalcitrant barn door until he pried it wide enough open to let him slip out. He had caught the scent, as Link predicted, and he had turned into the main street of Hampton a bare five minutes behind the carryall.

As he was on his orderly journey toward the Chatham home, Olive spied him from the dooryard and ran out to greet him.

54

And Eben Shunk, seeing them, waited only long enough to snatch up his rope and landing net, and gave chase. Coming upon the unsuspecting pair from behind, he was able to jam the net over Chum's head before the placidly pacing collie was aware of his presence.

Chum, catching belated sight and scent of his enemy, sought right valiantly to free himself and give battle. But the tough meshes of the net had been drawn as tightly over his head and jaws as any glove, holding him helpless. And Shunk was fastening the rope about the wildly struggling neck. It was then that Olive sprang to her canine comrade's aid, only to be slapped out of the way by the irate and overoccupied man. Whereat, she had fled for reinforcements.

A dog has but a single set of weapons, namely, his mighty jaws. The net held Chum's mouth fast shut. The noose was cutting off his wind. And bit by bit strangulation and confusion weakened the collie's struggles. With a final wrench of the noose, Shunk got under way. Heading down street toward his own alley, he dragged the fiercely unwilling prisoner behind him. A crowd accompanied him, as did their highly uncomplimentary remarks.

As Shunk reached the mouth of the alley and prepared to turn toward his own yard, two newcomers were added to the volunteer escort. But these two men were not content to look on in passive disgust. The elder of them hurled himself bodily at Shunk.

Link intervened as his enraged father-in-law was about to seize the dog catcher by the throat.

"Don't!" he warned, thrusting Chatham back. "There's the cop! You're a judge. You sure know a better way to get Shunk than to punch him. If you hit the man you give him a chance to sue. Do the suing, yourself!"

While he talked, Link was using his hastily drawn farm knife in scientific fashion. One slash severed the noose from about Chum's furry throat. A second cut parted the drawstring of the net. A dexterous tug at the meshes tore the net off the dog's head, setting free the terrible imprisoned jaws.

Meanwhile, choking back his craving to assail Shunk, Old Man Chatham strode up to the dumfounded constable.

"Officer," Chatham commanded in his very best bench manner, albeit still sputtering with rage and loss of breath, "you'll arrest that man—that Shunk person, there—and you'll convey him to the court room over my store. There I'll commit him to the calaboose to await a hearing in the morning."

Shunk gobbled in wordless and indignant dismay. The constable hesitated, confused.

55

"I accuse him," went on the grimly judicious accents, "of striking and knocking down my six-year-old daughter, Olive. He struck her, here, in the public thoroughfare, causing possible 'abrasions and contusions and mental and physical anguish,' as the statoot books describe it. The penalty for striking a minor, as you know, is severe. I shall press the charge, when the case comes before one of my feller magistrates, to-morrow. I shall also bring civil action for—"

"Hold on, there!" bleated Shunk as the constable, overawed by the array of legal terms, took a truculent step toward him. "Hold on, there! The brat—she beat at me with both her fists, she did, an'—"

"And in self-preservation against a six-year-old child you were obliged, to knock her down?" put in Link. "That's a plea that'll sure clear you. 'Specially if there's any of the jury that's got little girls of their own."

"I didn't knock nobody down!" fumed Shunk, wincing under the constable's grip on his shoulder. "She was a-pummellin' me an' tryin' to git the dog away from me. I just slapped her, light like, to make her quit. She slipped an' tumbled down. It didn't hurt her none. She was up an' off in a—"

"You'll all bear witness," observed Link, "that he confesses to hittin' the child and that she fell down when he hit her. We hadn't anything but her word to go on till now. And children are apt to get confused in court. Shunk, you've just saved us a heap of trouble by ownin' up."

"Ownin' up?" shrilled the dog catcher, stung to the belated fury which is supposed to obsess a cornered rat. "Ownin' up? Not much! Chatham, I'm a-goin' to bring soot agin you, as your child's legal gardeen, for her 'interferin' with an off'cer in pursoot of his dooty'! I'm a sworn off'cer of this borough. I was doin' my dooty in catchin' that unlicensed cur yonder. She interfered with me an' tried to git him away from me. I know enough law to—"

He checked himself, then pointed to Link and demanded:

"Constable Todd, I want you should arrest Lincoln Ferris! I charge him with assaultin' me, just now, in the presence of ev'ry one here an' interferin' with me in the pursoot of my dooty, an' for takin' away from me, with a drawn knife, an unlicensed dog I had caught as the law orders I should catch such dogs on the streets of this borough. Take him along unless you want to lose your shield for neglect of dooty. If I've got to stand trial, there's a couple of men who'll stand it too."

"Gee!" groaned Old Man Chatham, his legal lore revealing to him the mess wherein Shunk could so easily involve Ferris and

56

himself. "You were dead right, Link. One dog can cause more mixups in a c'munity than—"

"Than Eben Shunk?" asked Ferris. "No, you're wrong, sir. Shunk can stir up more bother than a poundful of dogs. Listen here, Shunk," he went on. "You claim that Olive and I both interfered with you in the pursuit of your duty. How did we?"

"By tryin' to take away from me a dog that the law c'mpelled me to catch, of course," snapped Eben, adding: "An' I charge you with 'sault and batt'ry too. You hit me in the stummick an' knocked me clean off'n the sidewalk."

"I was at work over my dog with one hand and I was holding back Mr. Chatham with the other," denied Link. "How could I have hit you? Did any one here see me strike this man?" he challenged the crowd.

"Aw, you didn't hit him!" answered one of the boys who had picked up stones. "He slipped on the curb. I saw him do it. Nobody hit him."

"That's right," agreed the constable. "I was here. And I didn't witness any assault."

"I'm thinkin' you'll have trouble provin' that assault charge, Shunkie," grinned Link. "Now for the other one. Judge," he said, addressing his worried father-in-law, "you are an authority on legal things. I grant it's a misdemeanour—or a crime—or something—to interfere with a dog catcher on a street of his own bailiwick when he's pullin' along an unlicensed dog. But what would the law be if Shunk had grabbed a duly licensed dog—a dog that was wearin' his license tag on his collar, like the law directs—a dog that was walkin' peacefully along the street, guardin' a child whose fam'ly it belonged to? Would that child or would the dog's owner be committin' any punishable fault for tryin' to keep the dog catcher from stealin' their pet? Would they? And would the dog catcher have any right to lay hands on such a dog? Would he have any case against such child or man? Hey?"

"Why, no! Of course not!" fumed Old Man Chatham. "He'd have no legal right to touch such a dog. They'd have a right to protect the beast from him. But that's all beside the point. The point is—"

"The point is," intervened Link, calling Chum to him by a snap of the fingers—"the point is that I was bothered by this man's threats to grab my dog and torture him. So I walked into town yesterday and paid my dollar license fee to the borough clerk and took out a license for Chum. I paid ten cents extra for a license tag and I fastened it on Chum's collar, as the law directs. See?"

57

He parted the heavy masses of ruff on the collie's throat, bringing to view a narrow circular collar, whereon dangled a little brass triangle.

At sight of the emblem Shunk's jaw dropped.

"I didn't see that!" he stammered aghast. "You told me last week he wa'n't licensed. How was I to know—"

"The borough clerk read me the law," replied Ferris. "The law commands that dog catchers search a dog's collar for license tags before taking him in charge. Shunkie, I'm afraid your sweet hopes of beatin' Chum to death must be folded up and laid away, like the pants of some dear dead friend. Something tells me, too, that the mayor and council will appoint a brand-new poundmaster when our complaint is laid before 'em and when they hear their champion dog catcher's in the hoosgow on a charge of beatin' a child. Something tells me, too, that you'll find it c'nvenient to move somewheres else, when you get out, and give some other burg the honour of havin' a Meanest Man in its 'mongst."

"If I'd 'a' cotched him a day earlier," moaned Shunk in utter regret and to himself rather than to the others—"if I'd—"

"You couldn't, Shunkie!" replied Link blithely. "I saw to that! He didn't stir off my land till I had time to come and get him licensed. If it hadn't been for holdin' back the judge, here, from wallopin' you, I wouldn't even of hurried to-day, when I found you had Chum. I was kind of hopin' you might try it. That's why I didn't head Chum off when I guessed he'd started for town. I was waitin' for you. That's why I got the license."

From his pocket Link fished out a soiled half sheet of paper and tendered it to the bulging-eyed dog catcher.

"Prop'ty of yours," he explained. "You let it drop out'n your coat that day you nosed round my farm lookin' for Chum. At the time I had an idea you was lookin' for a dollar fee. When I read that note I saw you was after a hundred-dollar fee—the cash you was offered by Sim Hooper if you could impound Chum and then let Sim sneak him out of your yard and over to Pat'son, to a collie dealer there, before I c'd come to redeem him.

"No wonder you was hoverin' round my farm like a buzzard that smells garbage! I showed that note to Mayor Wipple yest'day. So there's no need of you tearin' it all up like that, Shunkie. I figgered I might make it more amoosin' for you if I let you catch Chum before I sprung the note on you.

"I'm sure obleeged to you, Chum, son, for rollin' on his coat just when you happened to be able to roll that note out'n it. You're one wise pup!"

58

FOUR

The Tracker

The child's parents were going to Europe for three months, that winter. The child himself was getting over a nervous ailment. The doctors had advised he be kept out of school for a term; and be sent to the country.

His mother was afraid the constant travel from place to place, in Europe, might be too much for him. So she asked leave of the Mistress and the Master,—one of whom was her distant relative—for the convalescent to stay at the Place during his parents' absence.

That was how it all started.

The youngster was eleven years old; lank and gangling, and blest with a fretful voice and with far less discipline and manners than a three-month collie pup. His name was Cyril. Briefly, he was a pest,—an unspeakable pest.

For the first day or two at the Place, the newness of his surroundings kept Cyril more or less in bounds. Then, as homesickness and novelty alike wore off, his adventurous soul expanded.

He was very much at home;—far more so than were his hosts, and infinitely more pleased than they with the situation general. He had an infinite genius for getting into trouble. Not in the delightfully normal fashion of the average growing boy; but in furtively crafty ways that did not belong to healthy childhood.

Day by day, Cyril impressed his odd personality more and more on everything around him. The atmosphere of sweet peace which had brooded, like a blessing, over the whole Place, was dispersed.

The cook,—a marvel of culinary skill and of long service,—gave tearful warning, and departed. This when she found the insides of all her cooking utensils neatly soaped; and the sheaf of home-letters in her work-box replaced by cigar-coupons.

One of the workmen threw over his job with noisy blasphemy; when his room above the stables was invaded by stealth and a comic-paper picture of a goat's head substituted for his dead mother's photograph in the well-polished little bronze frame on his bureau.

And so on, all along the line.

59

The worst and most continuous sufferer from Cyril's loathed presence on the Place was the massive collie, Lad.

The child learned, on the first day of his visit, that it would be well-nigh as safe to play with a handful of dynamite as with Lad's gold-and-white mate, Lady. Lady did not care for liberties from any one. And she took no pains to mask her snappish first-sight aversion to the lanky Cyril. Her fiery little son, Wolf, was scarce less formidable than she, when it came to being teased by an outsider. But gallant old Lad was safe game.

He was safe game for Cyril, because Lad's mighty heart and soul were miles above the possibility of resenting anything from so pitifully weak and defenceless a creature as this child. He seemed to realise, at a glance, that Cyril was an invalid and helpless and at a physical disadvantage. And, as ever toward the feeble, his big nature went out in friendly protection to this gangling wisp of impishness.

Which was all the good it did him.

In fact, it laid the huge collie open to an endless succession of torment. For the dog's size and patience seemed to awaken every atom of bullying cruelty in the small visitor's nature.

Cyril, from the hour of his arrival, found acute bliss in making Lad's life a horror. His initial step was to respond effusively to the collie's welcoming advances; so long as the Mistress and the Master chanced to be in the room. As they passed out, the Mistress chanced to look back.

She saw Cyril pull a bit of cake from his pocket and, with his left hand, proffer it to Lad. The tawny dog stepped courteously forward to accept the gift. As his teeth were about to close daintily on the cake, Cyril whipped it back out of reach; and with his other hand rapped Lad smartly across the nose.

Had any grown man ventured a humiliating and painful trick of that sort on Lad, the collie would have been at the tormentor's throat, on the instant. But it was not in the great dog's nature to attack a child. Shrinking back, in amaze, his abnormally sensitive feelings jarred, the collie retreated majestically to his beloved "cave" under the music-room piano.

To the Mistress's remonstrance, Cyril denied most earnestly that he had done the thing. Nor was his vehemently tearful denial shaken by her assertion that she had seen it all.

Lad soon forgave the affront. And he forgave a dozen other and worse maltreatments which followed. But, at last, the dog took to shunning the neighbourhood of the pest. That availed him nothing; except to make Cyril seek him out in whatsoever refuge the dog had chosen.

60

Lad, trotting hungrily to his dinner dish, would find his food thick-strewn with cayenne pepper or else soaked in reeking gasoline.

Lad, seeking peace and solitude in his piano cave, would discover his rug, there, cleverly scattered with carpet tacks, points upward.

Lad, starting up from a snooze at the Mistress's call, would be deftly tripped as he started to bound down the veranda steps, and would risk bruises and fractures by an ugly fall to the driveway below.

Wherever Lad went, whatever Lad did, there was a cruel trick awaiting him. And, in time, the dog's dark eyes took on an expression of puzzled unhappiness that went straight to the hearts of the two humans who loved him.

All his life, Lad had been a privileged character on the Place. Never had he known nor needed whip or chain. Never had he,—or any of the Place's other dogs,—been wantonly teased by any human. He had known, and had given, only love and square treatment and stanch friendliness. He had ruled as benevolent monarch of the Place's Little People; had given leal service to his two deities, the Mistress and the Master; and had stood courteously aloof from the rest of mankind. And he had been very, very happy.

Now, in a breath, all this was changed. Ever at his heels, ever waiting to find some new way to pester him, was a human too small and too weak to attack;—a human who was forever setting the collie's highstrung nerves on edge or else actively hurting him. Lad could not understand it. And as the child gained in health and strength, Lad's lot grew increasingly miserable.

The Mistress and the Master were keenly aware of conditions. And they did their best,—a useless best,—to mitigate them for the dog. They laboured over Cyril, to make him leave Lad alone. They pointed out to him the mean cowardice of his course of torture. They even threatened to send him to nearer relatives until his parents' return. All in vain. Faced with the most undeniable proofs, the child invariably would lie. He denied that he had ever ill-used Lad in any way; and would weep, in righteous indignation, at the charges. What was to be done?

"I thought it would brighten up the house so, to have a child in it again!" sighed the Mistress as she and her husband discussed the matter, uselessly, for the fiftieth time, after one of these scenes. "I looked forward so much to his coming here! But he's—oh, he isn't like any child I ever heard of before!"

"If I could devote five busy minutes a day to him," grunted the Master, "with an axe-handle or perhaps a balestick—"

"You wouldn't do it!" denied his wife. "You wouldn't harm him; any more than Lad does. That's the trouble. If Cyril belonged to us, we could punish him. Not with a—a balestick, of course. But he needs a good wholesome spanking, more than any one else I can think of. That or some other kind of punishment that would make an impression on him. But what can we do? He isn't ours—"

"Thank God!" interpolated the Master, piously.

"And we can't punish other people's children," she finished. "I don't know what we can do. I wouldn't mind half so much about the other sneaky things he does; if it wasn't for the way he treats Laddie. I—"

"Suppose we send Lad to the boarding kennels, at Ridgewood, till the brat is gone?" suggested the Master. "I hate to do it. And the good old chap will be blue with homesickness there. But at least he'll get kind treatment. When he comes over to me and looks up into my eyes in that terribly appealing way, after Cyril has done some rotten thing to him,—well, I feel like a cur, not to be able to justify his faith that I can make things all right for him. Yes, I think I'll send him to the boarding kennels. And, if it weren't for leaving you alone to face things here, I'd be tempted to hire a stall at the kennels for myself, till the pest is gone."

The next day, came a ray of light in the bothered gloom. And the question of the boarding kennels was dropped. The Mistress received a letter from Cyril's mother. The European trip had been cut short, for business reasons; and the two travellers expected to land in New York on the following Friday.

"Who dares say Friday is an unlucky day?" chortled the Master in glee, as his wife reached this stage of the letter.

"And," the Mistress read on, "we will come out to the Place, on the noon train; and take darling Cyril away with us. I wish we could stay longer with you; but Henry must be in Chicago on Saturday night. So we must catch a late afternoon train back to town, and take the night train West. Now, I—"

"Most letters are a bore," interpolated the Master. "Or else they're a bother. But this one is a pure rapture. Read it more slowly, won't you, dear? I want to wallow in every blessèd word of hope it contains. Go ahead. I'm sorry I interrupted. Read on. You'll never have such another enthusiastic audience."

"And now," the Mistress continued her reading, "I am going to ask both of you not to say a single word to precious Cyril about our coming home so soon. We want to surprise him. Oh, to think what his lovely face will be like, when he sees us walking in!"

"And to think what my lovely face will be like, when I see him walking out!" exulted the Master. "Laddie, come over here. We've got the gorgeousest news ever! Come over and be glad!"

Lad, at the summons, came trotting out of his cave, and across the room. Like every good dog who has been much talked to, he was as adept as any dead-beat in reading the varying shades of the human voice. The voices and faces alike of his two adored deities told him something wonderful had happened. And, as ever, he rejoiced in their gladness. Lifting his magnificent head, he broke into a salvo of trumpeting barks;—the oddly triumphant form of racket he reserved for great moments.

"What's Laddie doing?" asked Cyril, from the threshold. "He sounds as if he was going mad or something."

"He's happy," answered the Mistress.

"Why's he happy?" queried the child.

"Because his Master and I are happy," patiently returned the Mistress.

"Why are you happy?" insisted Cyril.

"Because to-day is Thursday," put in the Master. "And that means to-morrow will be Friday."

"And on Friday," added the Mistress, "there's going to be a beautiful surprise for you, Cyril. We can't tell you what it is, but—"

"Why can't you tell me?" urged the child. "Aw, go ahead and tell me! I think you might."

The Master had gone over to the nearest window; and was staring out into the grey-black dusk. Midwinter gripped the dead world; and the twilight air was deathly chill. The tall naked treetops stood gaunt and wraithlike against a leaden sky.

To the north, the darkness was deepest. Evil little puffs of gale stirred the powdery snow into myriads of tiny dancing white devils. It had been a fearful winter, thus far; colder than for a score of years; so cold that many a wild woodland creature, which usually kept far back in the mountains, had ventured down nearer to civilisation for forage and warmth.

Deer tracks a-plenty had been seen, close up to the gates of the Place. And, two days ago, in the forest, half a mile away, the Master had come upon the half-human footprints of a young bear. Starvation stalked abroad, yonder in the white hills. And need for provender had begun to wax stronger among the folk of the wilderness than their inborn dread of humans.

"There's a big snowstorm coming up," ruminated the Master, as he scanned the grim weather-signs. "A blizzard, perhaps. I—I hope it won't delay any incoming steamers. I hope at least one of them will dock on schedule. It—"

He turned back from his musings, aware for the first time that a right sprightly dialogue was going on. Cyril was demanding for the eighth time:

"Why won't you tell me? Aw, I think you might! What's going to happen that's so nice, Friday?"

"Wait till Friday and see," laughed the Mistress.

"Shucks!" he snorted. "You might tell me, now. I don't want to wait and get s'prised. I want to know now. Tell me!"

Under her tolerant smile, the youngster's voice scaled to an impatient whine. He was beginning to grow red.

"Let it go at that!" ordained the Master. "Don't spoil your own fun, by trying to find out, beforehand. Be a good sportsman."

"Fun!" snarled Cyril. "What's the fun of secrets? I want to know—"

"It's snowing," observed the Mistress, as a handful of flakes began to drift past the windows, tossed along on a puff of wind.

"I want to know!" half-wept the child; angry at the change of subject, and noting that the Mistress was moving toward the next room, with Lad at her heels. "Come back and tell me!"

He stamped after her to bar her way. Lad was between the irate Cyril and the Mistress. In babyish rage at the dog's placid presence in his path, he drew back one ungainly foot and kicked the astonished collie in the ribs.

At the outrage, Lad spun about, a growl in his throat. But he forbore to bite or even to show his teeth. The growl had been of indignant protest at such unheard-of treatment; not a menace. Then the dog stalked haughtily to his cave, and lay down there.

But the human witnesses to the scene were less forbearing;— being only humans. The Mistress cried out, in sharp protest at the little brute's action. And the Master leaned forward, swinging Cyril clear of the ground. Holding the child firmly, but with no roughness, the Master steadied his own voice as best he could; and said:

"This time you've not even bothered to wait till our backs were turned. So don't waste breath by crying and saying you didn't do it. You're not my child; so I have no right to punish you. And I'm not going to. But I want you to know you've just kicked something that's worth fifty of you."

"You let me down!" Cyril snarled.

"Lad is too white and clean and square to hurt anything that can't hit back," continued the Master. "And you are not. That's the difference between you. One of the several million differences,—all of them in Lad's favour. When a child begins life by being cruel to dumb animals, it's a pretty bad sign for the way he's due to treat his fellow-humans in later years,—if ever any of them are at his mercy. For your own sake, learn to behave at least as decently as a dog. If"

"You let me down, you big bully!" squalled Cyril, bellowing with impotent fury. "You let me down! I—"

"Certainly," assented the Master, lowering him to the floor. "I didn't hurt you. I only held you so you couldn't run out of the room, before I'd finish speaking; as you did, the time I caught you putting red pepper on Lad's food. He—"

"You wouldn't dare touch me, if my folks were here, you big bully!" screeched the child, in a veritable mania of rage; jumping up and down and actually foaming at the mouth. "But I'll tell 'em on you! See if I don't! I'll tell 'em how you slung me around and said I was worse'n a dirty dog like Lad. And Daddy'll lick you for it. See if he don't! He—"

The Master could not choke back a laugh; though the poor Mistress looked horribly distressed at the maniac outburst, and strove soothingly to check it. She, like the Master, remembered now that Cyril's doting mother had spoken of the child's occasional fits of red wrath. But this was the first glimpse either of them had had of these. Hitherto, craft had served Cyril's turn better than fury.

At sound of the Master's unintentional laugh the unfortunate child went quite beside himself in his transport of rage.

"I won't stay in your nasty old house!" he shrieked. "I'm going to the very first house I can find. And I'm going to tell 'em how you hammered a little feller that hasn't any folks here to stick up for him. And I'll get 'em to take me in and send a tel'gram to Daddy and Mother to come save me. I—"

To the astonishment of both his hearers, Cyril broke off chokingly in his yelled tirade; caught up a bibelot from the table, hurled it with all his puny force at Lad, the innocent cause of the fracas, and then rushed from the room and from the house.

The Mistress stared after him, dumbfounded; his howls and the jarring slam of the house door echoing direfully in her ears. It was the Master who ended the instant's hush of amaze.

"Whenever I've heard a grown man say he wished he was a boy again," he mused, "I always set him down for a liar. But, for once in my life, I honestly wish I was a boy, once more. A boy one day younger and one inch shorter and one pound lighter than Cyril. I'd follow him out of doors, yonder, and give him the thrashing of his sweet young life. I'd—"

"Oh, do call him back!" begged the Mistress. "He'll catch his death of cold, and—"

"Why will he?" challenged the Master, without stirring. "For

65

all his noble rage, I noticed he took thought to grab up his cap and his overcoat from the hall, as he wafted himself away. And he still had his arctics on, from this afternoon. He won't—"

"But suppose he should really go over to one of the neighbours," urged the Mistress, "and tell such an awful story as he threatened to? Or suppose—"

"Not a chance!" the master reassured her. "Now that the summer people are away, there isn't an occupied house within half a mile of here. And he's not going to trudge a half-mile through the snow, in this bitter cold, for the joy of telling lies. No, he's down at the stables or else he's sneaked in through the kitchen; the way he did that other time when he made a grandstand exit after I'd ventured to lecture him on his general rottenness. Remember how worried about him you were, that time; till we found him sitting in the kitchen and pestering the maids? He—"

"But that time, he was only sulky," said the Mistress. "Not insanely angry, as he is now. I do hope—"

"Stop worrying!" adjured the Master. "He's all right."

Which proved, for perhaps the trillionth time in history, that a woman's intuitions are better worth following than a man's saner logic. For Cyril was not all right. And, at every passing minute he was less and less all right; until presently he was all wrong.

For the best part of an hour, in pursuance of her husband's counsel, the Mistress sat and waited for the prodigal's return. Then, surreptitiously, she made a round of the house; sent a man to ransack the stables, telephoned to the gate lodge, and finally came into the Master's study, big-eyed and pale.

"He isn't anywhere around," she reported, frightened. "It's dinner time. He's been gone an hour. Nobody's seen him. He isn't on the Place. Oh, I wonder if—"

"H'm!" grumbled her husband. "He's engineering an endurance contest, eh? Well, if he can stand it, we can."

But at sight of the deepening trouble in his wife's face, he got up from his desk. Going out into the hall, he summoned Lad.

"We might shout our heads off," he said, "and he'd never answer; if he's really trying to scare us. That's part of his lovable nature. There's just one way to track him, in double time. Lad!"

The Master had been drawing on his mackinaw and hip-boots as he spoke. Now he opened the front door.

"Laddie!" he said, very slowly and incisively to the expectantly eager collie. "Cyril! Find Cyril! Find him!"

To the super-wise collie, there was nothing confusing in the command. Like many another good dog, he knew the humans of the household by their names; as well as did any fellow-human. And he knew from long experience the meaning of the word, "Find!"

Countless times that word had been used in games and in earnest. Its significance, now, was perfectly plain to him. The master wanted him to hunt for the obnoxious child who so loved to annoy and hurt him.

Lad would rather have found any one else, at the Master's behest. But it did not occur to the trained collie to disobey. With a visible diminishing of his first eager excitement, but with submissive haste, the big dog stepped out on to the veranda and began to cast about in the drifts at the porch edge.

Immediately, he struck Cyril's shuffling trail. And, immediately, he trotted off along the course.

The task was less simple than ordinarily. For, the snow was coming down in hard-driven sheets; blotting out scent almost as effectively as sight. But not for naught had a thousand generations of Lad's thoroughbred ancestors traced lost sheep through snowstorms on the Scottish moors. To their grand descendant they had transmitted their weird trailing power, to the full. And the scent of Cyril, though faint and fainter, and smothered under swirling snow, was not too dim for Lad's sensitive nostrils to catch and hold it.

The Master lumbered along, through the rising drifts, as fast as he could. But the way was rough and the night was as black dark as it was cold. In a few rods, the dog had far outdistanced him. And, knowing how hard must be the trail to follow by sense of smell, he forbore to call back the questing collie, lest Lad lose the clue altogether. He knew the dog was certain to bark the tidings when he should come up with the fugitive.

The Master by this time began to share his wife's worry. For the trail Lad was following led out of the grounds and across the highway, toward the forest.

The newborn snowstorm was developing into a very promising little blizzard. And the icy lash of the wind proved the fallacy of the old theory, "too cold to snow." Even by daylight it would have been no light task to steer a true course through the whirling and blinding storm. In the darkness the man found himself stumbling along with drunkenly zigzag steps; his buffeted ears strained through the noise of the wind for sound of Lad's bark.

But no such sound came to him. And, he realised that snow and adverse winds can sometimes muffle even the penetrating bark of a collie. The man grew frightened. Halting, he shouted with all the power of his lungs. No whimper from Cyril answered the hail.

Nor, at his Master's summons, did Lad come bounding back through the drifts. Again and again, the Master called.

For the first time in his obedient life, Lad did not, respond to the call. And the Master knew his own voice could not carry, for a single furlong, against wind and snowfall.

"I'll go on for another half-hour," he told himself, as he sought to discern the dog's all-but obliterated footsteps through the deepening snow. "And then I'll go back and raise a search party."

He came to a bewildered stop. Fainter and more indistinguishable had Lad's floundering tracks become. Now,—by dint of distance and snow,—they ceased to be visible in the welter of drifted whiteness under the glare of the Master's flashlight.

"This means a search party," decided the man.

And he turned homeward, to telephone for a posse of neighbours.

Lad, being only a dog, had no such way of sharing his burden. He had been told to find the child. And his simple code of life and of action left him no outlet from doing his duty; be that duty irksome or easy. So he kept on. Far ahead of the Master, his keen ears had not caught the sound of the shouts. The gale and the snow muffled them and drove them back into the shouter's throat.

Cyril, naturally, had not had the remotest intent of labouring through the bitter cold and the snow to the house of any neighbour; there to tell his woful tale of oppression. The semblance of martyrdom, without its bothersome actuality, was quite enough for his purpose. Once before, at home, when his father had administered a mild and much-needed spanking, Cyril had made a like threat; and had then gone to hide in a chum's home, for half a day; returning to find his parents in agonies of remorse and fear, and ready to load him with peace-offerings. The child saw no reason why the same tactics should not serve every bit as triumphantly, in the present case.

He knew the maids were in the kitchen and at least one man was in the stables. He did not want his whereabouts to be discovered before he should have been able to raise a healthy and dividend-bringing crop of remorse in the hearts of the Mistress and the Master, so he resolved to go farther afield.

In the back of the meadow, across the road, and on the hither side of the forest, was a disused cattle-barrack, with two stalls under its roofpile of hay. The barrack was one of Cyril's favourite playhouses. It was dry and tight. Through his thick clothing he was not likely to be very cold, there; for an hour or two. He could snuggle down in the warm hay and play Indians, with considerable

68

comfort; until such time as the fright and penitence of his hosts should have come to a climax and make his return an ovation.

Meanwhile, it would be fun to picture their uneasiness and fear for his safety; and to visualise their journeyings through the snow to the houses of various neighbours, in search of the lost child.

Buoyed up by such happy thoughts as these, Cyril struck out at a lively pace for the highroad and into the field beyond. The barrack, he knew, lay diagonally across the wide meadow, and near the adjoining woods. Five minutes of tramping through the snow ought to bring him to it. And he set off, diagonally.

But, before he had gone a hundred yards, he lost his first zest in the adventure. The darkness had thickened; and the vagrant wind-gusts had tightened into a steady gale;—a gale which carried before it a blinding wrack of stingingly hard-driven snow.

The grey of the dying dusk was blotted out. The wind smote and battered the spindling child. Mechanically, he kept on for five or six minutes, making scant and irregular progress. Then, his spirit wavered. Splendid as it would be to scare these hateful people, there was nothing splendid in the weather that numbed him with cold and took away his breath and half-blinded him with snow.

What was the fun of making others suffer; if he himself were suffering tenfold more? And, on reaching the barrack, he would have all that freezing and blast-hammering trip back again. Aw, what was the use?

And Cyril came to a halt. He had definitely abandoned his high enterprise. Turning around, he began to retrace his stumbling steps. But, at best, in a large field, in a blizzard and in pitch darkness, and with no visible landmarks, it is not easy to double back on one's route, with any degree of accuracy. In Cyril's case, the thing was wholly impossible.

Blindly he had been travelling in an erratic half-circle. Another minute of walking would have brought him to the highroad, not far from the Place's gateway. And, as he changed his course, to seek the road, he moved at an obtuse angle to his former line of march.

Thus, another period of exhausting progress brought him up with a bump against a solid barrier. His chilled face came into rough contact with the top rail of a line fence.

So relieved was the startled child by this encounter that he forgot to whine at the abrasion wrought upon his cheek by the rail. He had begun to feel the first gnawings of panic. Now, at once, he was calm again. For he knew where he was. This was the line fence between the Place's upper section and the land of the next neighbour. All he need do was to walk along in the shelter of it, touching the rails now and then to make certain of not straying, until he should come out on the road, at the gate lodge. It was absurdly easy; compared to what he had been undergoing. Besides, the lee of the fence afforded a certain shelter from wind and snow. The child realised he had been turned about in the dark; and had been going in the wrong direction. But now, at last, his course seemed plain to him.

So he set off briskly, close to the fence;—and directly away from the nearby road.

For another half-hour he continued his inexplicably long tramp; always buoyed up by the hope of coming to the road in a few more steps; and doggedly sure of his bearings. Then, turning out from the fence, in order to skirt a wide hazel thicket, he tripped over an outcrop of rock, and tumbled into a drift. Getting to his feet, he sought to regain the fence; but the fall had shaken his senses and he floundered off in the opposite direction. After a rod or two of such futile plunging, a stumbling step took him clean off the edge of the world, and into the air.

All this, for the merest instant. Then, he landed with a jounce in a heap of brush and dead leaves. Squatting there, breathless, he stretched out his mittened hand, along the ground. At the end of less than another yard of this exploring, his fingers came again to the edge of the world and were thrust out over nothingness.

With hideous suddenness, Cyril understood where he was; and what had happened to him and why. He knew he had followed the fence for a full mile, away from the road; through the nearer woods, and gradually upward until he had come to the line of hazels on the lip of the ninety-foot ravine which dipped down into a swamp-stretch known as "Pancake Hollow."

That was what he had done. In trying to skirt the hazels, he had stepped over the cliff-edge, and had dropped five feet or more to a rather narrow ledge that juts out over the ravine.

Well did he remember this ledge. More than once, on walks with the Mistress and the Master, he had paused to look down on it and to think what fun it would be to imprison some one there and to stand above, guying the victim. It had been a sweet thought. And now, he, himself, was imprisoned there.

But for luck, he might have fallen the whole ninety feet; for the ledge did not extend far along the face of the cliff. At almost any other spot his tumble might have meant—

Cyril shuddered a little; and pursued the grisly theme no further. He was safe enough, till help should come. And, here, the

70

blast of the wind did not reach him. Also, by cuddling low in the litter of leaves and fallen brush, he could ward off a little of the icy cold.

He crouched there; shaking and worn out. He was only eleven. His fragile body had undergone a fearful hour of toil and hardship. As he was drawing in his breath for a cry to any chance searchers, the boy was aware of a swift pattering, above his head. He looked up. The sky was a shade or two less densely black than the ravine edge. As Cyril gazed in terror, a shaggy dark shape outlined itself against the sky-line, just above him.

Having followed the eccentric footsteps of the wanderer, with great and greater difficulty, to the fence-lee where the tracing was much easier, Lad came to the lip of the ravine a bare five minutes after the child's drop to the ledge.

There, for an instant, the great dog stood; ears cocked, head inquiringly on one side; looking down upon the ledge. Cyril shrank to a quivering little heap of abject terror, at sight of the indistinct animal shape looming mountain-high above him.

This for the briefest moment. Then back went Lad's head in a pealing bark that seemed to fill the world and to re-echo from a myriad directions at once. Again and again, Lad gave clamorous voice to his discovery of the lost child.

On a clear or windless night, his racket must have penetrated to the dullest ears at the Place, and far beyond. For the bark of a dog has more carrying power than has any other sound of double its volume. But, in the face of a sixty-mile gale laden with tons of flying snow, the report of a cannon could scarce have carried over the stretch of windswept ground between the ravine and the Place.

Lad seemed to understand this. For, after a dozen thunderous barks, he fell silent; and stood again, head on one side, in thought.

At first sound of the barking, Cyril had recognised the dog. And his terror had vanished. In its place surged a peevish irritation against the beast that had so frightened him. He groped for a rock-fragment to hurl up at the rackety collie.

Then, the child paused in his fumbling. The dog had scant reason to love him or to seek his society. Of late, Lad had kept out of his way as much as possible. Thus it was not likely the collie had come here of his own accord, on such a night; for the mere joy of being with his tormentor.

His presence must mean that the Master was close behind; and that the whole Place was in a ferment of anxiety about the wanderer. By stoning Lad away and checking the barks, Cyril might well prevent the searchers from finding him. Too weak and too numb with cold to climb up the five-foot cliff-face to the level ground above, he did not want to miss any chance for rescue.

Hence, as Lad ceased to bark, the child set up a yell, with all his slight lung-power, to attract the seekers' notice. He ordered Lad to "Speak!" and shook his fist angrily at the dog, when no answering bark followed.

Despairing of making any one hear his trumpeting announcement that he had found the child, Lad presently made up his mind as to the only course that remained. Wheeling about, head down, he faced the storm again; and set off at what speed he could compass, toward home, to lead the Master to the spot where Cyril was trapped. This seemed the only expedient left. It was what he had done, long ago, when Lady had caught her foot in a fox-trap, back in the woods.

As the dog vanished from against the grey-black skyline, Cyril set up a howl of wrathful command to him to come back. Anything was better than to be in this dreary spot alone. Besides, with Lad gone, how could Lad's Master find the way to the ledge?

Twice the child called after the retreating collie. And, in another few steps, Lad had halted and begun to retrace his way toward the ledge.

He did not return because of Cyril's call. He had learned, by ugly experience, to disregard the child's orders. They were wont to mean much unpleasantness for him. Nevertheless, Lad halted. Not in obedience to the summons; but because of a sound and a scent that smote him as he started to gallop away. An eddy of the wind had borne both to the dog's acute senses.

Stiffening, his curved eyeteeth baring themselves, his hackles bristling, Lad galloped back to the ravine-lip; and stood there sniffing the icy air and growling deep in his throat. Looking down to the ledge he saw Cyril was no longer its sole occupant. Crouched at the opening of a crevice, not ten feet from the unseeing child, was something bulky and sinister;—a mere menacing blur against the darker rock.

Crawling home to its lair, supperless and frantic with hunger, after a day of fruitless hunting through the dead forest world, a giant wildcat had been stirred from its first fitful slumber in the ledge's crevice by the impact of the child upon the heap of leaves. The human scent had startled the creature and it had slunk farther back into the crevice. The more so when the bark and inimical odour of a big dog were added to the shattering of the ravine's solitude.

Then the dog had gone away. Curiosity,—the besetting trait of

72

the cat tribe,—had mastered the crevice's dweller. The wildcat had wriggled noiselessly forward a little way, to learn what manner of enemy had invaded its lair. And peering out, it had beheld a spindling child; a human atom without strength or weapon.

Fear changed to fury in the bob-cat's feline heart. Here was no opponent; but a mere item of prey. And, with fury, stirred long-unsatisfied hunger; the famine hunger of midwinter which makes the folk of the wilderness risk capture or death by raiding guarded hencoops.

Out from the crevice stole the wildcat. Its ears were flattened close to its evil head. Its yellow eyes were mere slits of fire. Its claws unsheathed themselves from the furry pads,—long, hooked claws, capable of disembowelling a grown deer at one sabre-stroke of the muscular hindlegs. Into the rubble and litter of the ledge the claws sank, and receded, in rhythmic motion.

The compact yellow body tightened into a ball. The back quivered. The feet braced themselves. The cat was gauging its distance and making ready for a murder-spring. Cyril, his head turned the other way, was still peering up along the cliff-edge for sight of Lad.

This was what Lad's scent and hearing,—and perhaps something else,—had warned him of, in that instant of the wind's eddying shift. And this was the scene he looked down upon, now, from the ravine-lip, five feet above.

The collie brain,—though never the collie heart,—is wont to flash back, in moments of mortal stress, to the ancestral wolf. Never in his own life had Sunnybank Lad set eyes on a wildcat. But in the primal forests, wolf and bob-cat had perforce met and clashed, a thousand times. There they had begun and had waged the eternal cat-and-dog feud, of the ages.

Ancestry now told Lad that there is perhaps no more murderously dangerous foe than an angry wildcat. Ancestry also told him a wolf's one chance of certain victory in such a contest. Ancestry's aid was not required, to tell him the mortal peril awaiting this human child who had so grievously and causelessly tormented him. But the great loyal heart, in this stark moment, took no thought of personal grudges. There was but one thing to do,—one perilous, desperate chance to take; if the child were to be saved.

The wildcat sprang.

Such a leap could readily have carried it across double the space which lay between it and Cyril. But not one-third of that space was covered in the lightning pounce.

From the upper air—apparently from nowhere—a huge shaggy

73

body launched itself straight downward. As unerringly as the swoop of an eagle, the down-whizzing bulk flew. It smote the leaping wildcat, in mid-flight.

A set of mighty jaws,—jaws that could crack a beef-bone as a man cracks a filbert,—clove deep and unerringly into the cat's back, just behind the shoulders. And those jaws flung all their strength into the ravening grip.

A squall—hideous in its unearthly clangour—split the night silences. The maddened cat whirled about, spitting and yowling; and set its foaming teeth in the dog's fur-armoured shoulder. But before the terrible curved claws could be called into action, Lad's rending jaws had done their work upon the spine.

To the verge of the narrow ledge the two combatants had rolled in their unloving embrace. Its last lurch of agony carried the stricken wildcat over the edge and out to the ninety-foot drop into the ravine. Lad was all-but carried along with his adversary. He clawed wildly with his toes for a purchase on the smooth cliff wall; over which his hindquarters had slipped. For a second he hung, swaying, above the abyss.

Cyril, scared into semi-insanity by sight of the sudden brief battle, had caught up a stick from the rubbish at his feet. With this, not at all knowing what he did, he smote the struggling Lad over the head with every atom of his feeble force.

Luckily for the gallant dog, the stick was rotten. It broke, in the blow; but not before its impact had well-nigh destroyed Lad's precarious balance.

One clawing hindfoot found toe-room in a flaw of rock. A tremendous heave of all his strained muscles; and Lad was scrambling to safety on the ledge.

Cyril's last atom of vigour and resistance had gone into that panic blow at the dog. Now, the child had flung himself helplessly down, against the wall of the ledge; and was weeping in delirious hysterics.

Lad moved over to him; hesitated a moment, looking wistfully upward at the solid ground above. Then, he seemed to decide which way his duty pointed. Lying down beside the freezing child, he pressed his great shaggy body close to Cyril's; protecting him from the swirling snow and from the worst of the cold.

The dog's dark, deep-set eyes roved watchfully toward the crevice, alert for sign of any other marauder that might issue forth. His own shaggy shoulder was hurting him, annoyingly, from the wildcat's bite. But to this he gave no heed. Closer yet, he pressed his warm, furry body to the ice-cold youngster; fending off the elements as valorously as he had fended off the wildcat.

The warmth of the great body began to penetrate Cyril's numbed senses. The child snuggled to the dog gratefully. Lad's pink tongue licked caressingly at the white face; and the collie whimpered crooning sympathy to the little sufferer.

So, for a time the dog and the child lay there; Cyril's numb body warming under the contact.

Then, at a swift intake of the windy air, Lad's whimper changed to a thunder of wild barking. His nostrils had told him of the search party's approach, a few hundred yards to the windward.

Their dispiritingly aimless hunt changing into a scrambling rush in the direction whence came the faint-heard barks, the searchers trooped toward the ledge.

"Here we are!" shrilled the child, as the Master's halloo sounded directly above. "Here we are! Down here! A—a lion tackled us, awhile back. But we licked him;—I and Laddie!"

75

FIVE

"Youth Will be Served!"

Bruce was a collie—physically and in many other ways a super-collie. Twenty-six inches at the shoulder, seventy-five pounds in weight, his great frame had no more hint of coarseness than had his classic head and foreface.

His mighty coat was black-stippled at its edges, like Seedley Stirling's, giving the dog almost the look of a "tricolour" rather than of a "dark-sable-and-white." There was an air of majesty, of perfect breeding, about Bruce—an intangible something that lent him the bearing of a monarch. He was, in brief, such a dog as one sees perhaps thrice in a generation.

At the Place, after old Lad's death, Bruce ruled as king. He was no mere kennel dog—reared and cared for like some prize ox—but was part and parcel of the household, a member of the family, as befitted a dog of his beauty and brain and soul.

It was when Bruce was less than a year old that he was taken to his first A.K.C. bench show. The Master was eager that the dog-show world should acclaim his grand young dog, and that the puppy—like the youthful knights of old—should have fair chance to prove his mettle against the paladins of his kind. For it is in these shows that a dog's rating is determined; that he is pitted against the best in dogdom, before judges who are almost always competent and still oftener honest in their decisions.

The goal of the show dog is the championship, whose fifteen points must be annexed under no less than three judges, at three different times; in ratings that range from one point to five points, according to the number of dogs exhibited. To only the show's best dog of his or her special breed and sex are points awarded.

The Master took Bruce to his first A.K.C. show with much trepidation. He knew how perfect was this splendid young collie of his. But he also knew that the judge might turn out to be some ultra-modernist who preferred daintiness of head and smallness of bone and borzoi fore-face, to Bruce's wealth of bone and thickness of coat and unwonted size.

Modestly, therefore, he entered his dog only in the puppy and novice classes, and strove to cure his own show-ague by ceaseless grooming and rubbing and dandy-brushing of the youngster, whose burnished coat already stood out like a Circassian beauty's hair and who was fit in every way to make the showing of his life.

In intervals of polishing the bored puppy's coat, the Master spent much time in studying covertly the collie judge, who was chatting with a group of friends at the ring's edge, waiting for his breed's classes to be called.

The Master was partly puzzled, partly reassured, by the aspect of the little judge.

Angus McGilead's Linlithgow birth was still apparent in the very faintest burr of his speech and in the shrewd, pale eyes that peered, terrier-like, above his lean face and huge thatch of grizzling red beard. He was a man whose forebears had known collies as they knew their own children, and who rated a true collie above all mere money price.

From childhood McGilead had made a life study of this, his favourite breed. As a result, he was admittedly the chief collie authority on either side of the grey ocean. This fact, and his granite honesty, made him a judge to be looked up to with a reverent faith which had in it a tinge of fear.

Such was the man who, at this three-point show, was to pass judgment on Bruce.

After an eternity of waiting, the last airedale was led from the judging ring. The first collie class, "Puppies, male," was chalked on the blackboard. The Master, with one final ministration of the dandy-brush, snapped a ring-leash on Bruce's collar, and led him down the collie section into the ring.

Four other puppies were already there. McGilead, his shrewd pale eyes half shut, was lounging in one end of the enclosure, apparently listening to something the ring-steward was saying, but with his seemingly careless gaze and his keen mind wholly absorbed in watching the little procession of pups as it filed into the ring. Under the sandy lashes, his eyes caressed or censured all the entrants in turn, boring into their very souls.

Then, as the last of the five walked in and the gate was shut behind them, he came to life. Approaching the huddle of dogs and their handlers, he singled out a shivering little puppy whose baby fur had not yet been lost in the rough coat of maturity and whose body was still pudgy and formless.

"How old is this pup?" he asked the woman who was tugging at the boundingly excited baby's leash.

"Six months, yesterday!" was the garrulous answer. "Isn't he a little beauty, Judge? Two days younger and he'd have been too young to show. He just comes in the law. It's lucky he wasn't born two days later."

"No," gently contradicted McGilead, petting the downy little chap. "It's unlucky. Both for you and for him. The rules admit a pup to the show ring at six months. The rules are harsh, for they make him compete with dogs almost double his age. The puppy limit is from six to twelve months in shows. I don't want you to feel bad when I refuse to judge this little fellow. It isn't your fault, nor his, that he hasn't begun to develop. But it would be like putting a child of five into competitive examination at school with a lad of twenty."

Motioning her gently to a far corner, he rasped at the others. "Walk your dogs, please!"

The procession started around the ring. Presently, McGilead waved the Master to take Bruce to one side. Then he placed one after another of the remaining dogs on the central block and went over them with infinite care. At the end of the inspection, he beckoned the worried Master to bring Bruce to the block. After running his hands lightly over and under the pup, he turned to the ring-steward, who stood waiting with a ledger and a handful of ribbons.

Writing down four numbers in the book, McGilead took a blue and a red and a yellow and a white ribbon and advanced again toward the waiting exhibitors.

(And this, by the way, is the Big Moment, to any dog handler—this instant when the judge is approaching with the ribbons. For sheer thrill, it makes roulette and horse-racing seem puerile.)

To the Master, the little judge handed the blue ribbon. Then he awarded the red "second" and the yellow "third" and the white "reserve" to three others.

The recipient of the reserve snorted loudly.

"Say!" he complained. "Better judges than you have said this pup of mine is the finest collie of his age in America. What do you mean by giving him a measly reserve? What's the matter with him?"

"Compared with what's the matter with you," drawled McGilead, unruffled, "there's nothing at all the matter with him. Didn't anybody ever tell you how unsportsmanlike it is to argue a judge's decision in the ring? It's against the A.K.C. rules, too. I'm always glad, later, to explain my rulings to any one who asks me civilly. Since you want to know what's the matter with your dog, I'll tell you. He has spaniel ears. Fault number one. He is cow-hocked. Fault number two. He is apple-domed, and he's cheeky and he has a snipe-nose. Faults three, four and five. He's long-bodied and swaybacked and over-shot and his undercoat is as thin as your own sportsmanship. He carries his tail high over his back, too. And his outer coat is almost curly. Those are all the faults I can see about him just now. He'll never win anything in any A.K.C. show. It's only fair to tell you that; to save you further money and to save you from another such dirty breach of sportsmanship. That's all."

The Master, covertly petting Bruce and telling him in a whisper what a grand dog he was, waited at an end of the ring for the next class—"the novice"—to be called.

Here the competition was somewhat keener. Yet the result was the same. And Bruce found himself with another dark blue ribbon in token of his second victory.

Then, when the winning dogs of every class were brought into the ring for "Winners"—to decide on the best male collie,—Bruce received the winner's rosette, and found himself advanced three points on his fifteen-point journey toward the championship.

When the collie judging was over and the Master sat on the bench edge, petting his victorious dog, Angus McGilead strolled over to where the winner lay and stood staring down on him.

"How old?" he asked, curtly.

"Twelve months, next Tuesday," returned the Master.

"If he keeps on," pursued the dryly rasping voice, "you can say you own the greatest collie Angus McGilead has seen in ten years. It's a privilege to look at such a dog. A privilege. I'm not speaking, mind you, as the collie judge of this show, but as a man who has spent some fifty-odd years in studying the breed. I've not seen his like in many a day. I'll keep my eye on him."

And he was as good as his word. At every succeeding show to which the Master took Bruce, he was certain to run into McGilead, there as a spectator, standing with head on one side, brooding over the physical perfections of Bruce. Always the little judge was chary of his conversation with the Master. But always, he gazed upon Bruce as might an inspired artist on some still more inspired painting.

McGilead had been right in his prophecy as to the collie's future. Not only did Bruce "keep on," but the passing months added new wealth and lustre to his huge coat and new grace and shapeliness to his massive body, and a clearer and cleaner set of lines to his classic head.

Three more shows, two of them three-point exhibitions and one a single-pointer, brought him seven more points toward the championship. Then, on the day of the "Collie Club of the Union's" annual show, came the crowning triumph.

Thirty-two dogs were on hand, precisely the number, under the new rulings, to make it a five-point show. And Angus McGilead was the judge.

When McGilead gave Bruce the winner's rosette, which marked also his winning of the championship, the pale and shrewd old eyes were misted ever so little, and the hard and thin mouth was set like a gash.

It was as proud a moment in the little judge's life as in the Master's. America once more had a champion collie—a young dog at that—at which McGilead could point with inordinate pride, when collie-folk fell to bewailing the decadence of the breed in the Linlithgow man's adopted country.

"I gave him his first winners!" he bragged that night to a coterie of fellow countrymen, in a rare fit of expansiveness. "I gave him his first winners, first time ever he was showed. I said to myself when he swung into the ring that day—under twelve months old, mind you—I said: 'Angus, lad, yon's a dog!' I said. 'Watch him, Angus!' I said. 'For he's going far, is yon tike,' I said. And what's he done? Won his championship in five shows. In less'n a year. And I'm the man who gave him the 'winners' that got him his championship. Watch him! He's due to last for years longer and to clean up wherever he goes. Remember I said so, when you see him going through every bunch he's shown against. He's the grandest dog in America to-day, is Brucie."

Again was the Scotchman's forecast justified. At such few shows, during the next six years, as the Master found time to take him to, Bruce won prize after prize. Age did not seem to lessen his physical perfection. And the years added to the regal dignity that shone about him like an almost visible atmosphere.

Watching from the ring-side, or presiding in the ring Angus McGilead thrilled to the dog's every victory as to the triumph of some loved friend. There was an odd bond between the great dog and the little judge. Except for the Mistress and the Master, the collie felt scant interest in humanity at large. A one-man dog, he received the pettings of outsiders and the handling of judges with lofty coldness.

But, at sight of McGilead, the plumed tail was at once awag. The deepset eyes would soften and brighten, and the long nose would wrinkle into a most engaging smile. Bruce loved to be talked to and petted by Angus. He carried his affection for the inordinately tickled judge to the point of trying to shake hands with him or romp with him in the ring; to the outward scandal and inward delight of the sombre Scot.

"Can't you keep the beast from acting like he belonged to me, when I'm judging him?" grumpily complained McGilead, once to the Master. "A fine impression it makes, don't it, on strangers, when

80

they see him come wagging and grinning up to me and wanting to shake hands, or to roll over for me to play with him? One fool asked me, was it my own dog I gave the prize to. He said no outsider's dog would be making such a fuss over a judge. Try to keep him in better order in the ring, or I'll prove he isn't mine, by 'giving him the gate,' one of these days. See if I don't."

But he never did. And the Master knew well that he never would. So it was that Bruce's career as a winner continued unbrokenly, while other champions came and went.

With dogs, as with horses, youth will be served. By the time a horse is six, his racing days are past; and he has something like twenty years of cart or carriage mediocrity ahead of him. His glory as a track king has fled forever.

And with dogs—whose average life of activity runs little beyond ten years—ring honours usually come in youth or not at all. Yes, and they depart with youth. The dog remains handsome and useful for years thereafter. But his head has coarsened. His figure has lost its perfection. His gait stiffens. In a score of ways he drops back from the standard required of winners. Younger dogs are put above him. Which is life—whether in kennel, or in stable, or in office, or in the courts of love. Youth wins.

Yet the passing years seemed to take no perceptible toll of Bruce. His classic head lost none of its fineness. His body remained limber and graceful and shapely. His coat was mightier than ever. Even McGilead's apprehensive and super-piercing glance could find no flaw, no sign of oncoming age.

The years had, hitherto, been well-nigh as kind to Angus, himself. Dry and wiry and small, he had neither shown nor felt the weight of advancing age. Yet, now, passing his sixtieth milestone, an attack of rheumatic fever left him oddly heavy and slothful. Instead of taking the stairs two at a time, he set a foot on every step. And at the top of any very long flight, he was annoyed to find himself breathing absurdly hard.

He found himself, for the first time in his life, sneering at youth's gay ebullience, and snubbing the bumptiousness of his growing sons.

"Youth!" he snarled grimly once to the Master, as they met at a show. "Everything's for youth, these days. It was a-plenty different when I was young. Just as a man begins to get seasoned and to know his way around, folks call him an oldster and fix up a place for him in the chimney corner. Youth isn't the only thing in this world. Not by a long sight. Take Bruce, here, for instance. (Yes, I'm talking about you, you big ruffian! Give me your paw, now, and listen to me

81

tell how good you are!) Take Bruce, here, for instance. Nearly eight years old. Eight in August, isn't it? As old, that is, as fifty-odd for a human. And look at him! Is there one of the young bunch of dogs that can win against him—under any judge that knows his business? Not a one of 'em. He's finer to-day than he was when he came out at his first show. Us oldsters can still hold our own, and a little more. Bring on your youngsters! Me and Brucie are ready for 'em all. (Hey, Big Boy? Gimme your other paw, like a gentleman! Not the left one.) Why, first time I set eyes on this dog I said to myself—"

"I've got something up at The Place that's due to give Bruce the tussle of his life in the show ring some day," bragged the Master. "He's Bruce's own son, and grandson. That means he's pretty nearly seventy-five per cent. Bruce. And he shows it. His kennel name's 'Jock.' He's only eight months now, and he's the living image of what Bruce was at his age. Best head I ever saw. Great coat, too, and carriage. He's the best of all Bruce's dozens of pups, by far. I'm going to show him at the 'Charity' in September."

"Are you, though?" sniffed McGilead. "It happens I'm judging at the 'Charity.' (Some liars can say I'm beginning to show my age. But I take note they keep on wanting me to judge, oftener'n ever.) I'm judging at the 'Charity.' And I'll be on the lookout for that wonderful pup of yours. All pups are wonderful, I notice. Till they get in the ring. Being old Bruce's son, this youngster of yours can't be altogether bad. I grant that. But I'll gamble he'll never be what his Dad is."

"You'll have the first say-so on that," answered the Master. "I'm entering Bruce for 'Open, Any Colour,' at the 'Charity.' (By the way, it's the old fellow's last show. I'm going to retire him from the game while he's still good.) Little Jock is entered for 'Puppy and Novice.' It's a cinch they'll come together before you, in 'winners'!"

"And when they do," scoffed McGilead, "don't feel too bad if Bruce gets winners and the pup don't get a look in. Jock may never see a winners' class. Plenty of these promising world-beaters never do. You're as daft on this 'youth' notion as any of 'em. Here you've got the grandest collie in the States. And you turn your silly back on him and go cracking your jaw about an upstart pup of his that most likely has more flaws than fleas—and a bushel basketful of both. Grrh!"

Often, during the next three months, Angus found his mind dwelling reluctantly upon the newcomer. He was anxious to see the near-paragon. He realised he was all but prejudiced against the youngster by the Master's boastful praise.

Then, McGilead would pull himself up, short. For he prided

himself on his four-square honesty and his dearth of prejudice in show-ring matters. This absolute squareness had brought him where he was to-day—to the very foremost place among all dog-show judges. It had kept him respected and had kept his services in constant demand for decades, while showier and lesser judges had waxed and waned and had been forgotten.

This honesty of his was McGilead's fetish and pride in life. Yet, here he was, unsight, unseen, prejudiced against a dog, and that dog his adored Bruce's own son!

McGilead brought himself together, sharply, cursed himself for an old blackguard, and sought to put the whole matter out of his mind. Yet, somehow, he found himself looking forward to the five-point Charity show more interestedly than to any such event in years.

It was one of McGilead's myriad points of professional ethics never to go near the collie section of any show, until after his share of the judging should be over. Thus it was, on the day of the Charity show, his first glimpse of Jock was when the Master led the youngster into the ring, when the puppy class was called.

Six other pups also were brought into the ring. McGilead, as ever, surveyed them with breathless keenness, from between his half-shut eyes—pretending all the while to be talking interestedly with the ring-steward—while the procession filed in through the gate.

But his eyes, once singling out Jock, refused to focus on any other entrant. And he set his teeth in a twinge of wonder and admiration for the newcomer. Moreover, he observed in him none of the fright, or curiosity, or awkwardness that is the portion of so many puppies on their first entrance to the show-ring. The youngster seemed comfortably at home in the strange surroundings.

Nor was this unnatural. The Master had made use of a simple ruse that he had employed more than once before. Arriving at the show, long before the judging had begun, and while the first spectators were trailing in, he had led Jock at once to the ring, where, of course, neither the Master nor the dog had, technically, any right to be at such a time.

First unleashing Jock, the Master had let him roam at will for a few minutes around the strange enclosure; then had called the wandering collie over to him, fed him bits of fried liver and lured him into a romp. After which, the Master had sat down on the edge of the judging block, calling Jock to him, petting and feeding him for a few moments, and then persuading the pup to fall asleep at his feet.

83

Thus, when they re-entered the ring for the judging, Jock no longer regarded it as a strange and possibly terrifying abode. To him the ring was now a familiar and friendly place, where he had played and slept and been fed and made much of. All its associations were pleasant in the puppy's memory. And he was mildly pleased to be there again.

McGilead's veiled eyes were studying minutely every motion and every inch of Bruce's young son. And as a dog lover he rejoiced at what he saw. The pup was all the Master said and far more. Well-nigh as tall and as strong of frame as his sire, Jock had Bruce's classic head and wondrous coat; the older dog's perfect and short-backed body, ear carriage, flawless foreface, true collie expression and grace of action, soundness and build. Above all, Bruce had transmitted to him that same elusive air of regal dignity and nobility.

"Walk your dogs, please!" rasped the judge, starting out of his daze to a realisation that the seven exhibitors were waiting for him to come to earth again.

As, seven years earlier, he had waved Bruce aside, that he might not be bothered in his judging of the lesser contestants, so, now, he bade the Master take Jock into a corner while the parade and the preliminary examining went on. The Master—this time not worried—obeyed.

And the scene of Bruce's début was re-enacted, both in puppy and in novice classes. Not one competitor was worthy of a second's hesitancy between himself and Jock.

Then, for the time, the tawny débutante was allowed to go back in peace to his bench; and the other classes were called. When "Open, Any Colour," came up for judging, this most crucial of all classes had fine representation. Four sables, two tri-colours and two merles contested.

Yet, in all honesty, not one of the rest could equal old Bruce. The great dog stood forth, pre-eminently their superior. And, with the customary little tug of pleasure at his wizened heart, McGilead awarded to his old favourite the squarely earned blue ribbon.

"The pup's a wonder," he told himself. "But the old dog is still the best of the lot. The best of any lot."

The regular classes were judged; and the best dog in each came into the ring for winners. At last, Bruce and Jock stood side by side on the judging block. The contest had narrowed down to them.

And now, for the first time, McGilead was able to concentrate all his attention and his judging prowess on a comparison of the two. For several minutes he eyed them. He made their handlers shift the dogs' positions. He went over them, like an inspired surgeon, with his sensitive old fingers, though Bruce's body was already as familiar to his touch as is the keyboard to a pianist. He made them "show." He studied them from fifty angles.

Now, to casual observers, Angus McGilead was going through his task with a perfunctory deftness that verged on boredom. The tired, half-shut eyes and the wizened brown face gave no hint of emotion. Yet, within the Scotchman's heart, a veritable hell of emotion was surging.

This prolonged examination was not necessary. He had known it was not necessary from the first instant he had seen the two dogs, sire and son, standing side by side on the block before him. He was dragging out the judging, partly in the vain hope of finding something to make him reverse his first opinion, but chiefly to settle, one way or another, the battle that was waging within him.

For, at once, his acutely practised eye had discerned that Jock was the better dog. Not that he was better, necessarily, than Bruce had been a few years earlier. But hitherto unnoted marks of time on the older dog had sprung into sudden and merciless relief by comparison with the flawless youngster.

Seen alone, or with the average opponent, these would not have been noticeable. But alongside of Jock, the latter's perfection brought out every incipient flaw of age in his sire.

All this had been patent to McGilead at his first critical glance. The younger dog was the better. Only a shade the better, thus far, it is true. But by such shades are contests won—and lost.

No outsider—few professional judges—could have recognised the superiority of one of the competitors over the other. Yet McGilead recognised it as clearly as by lightning flare. And he saw his duty—the duty that lay plain before him.

He had given Bruce his earliest ring award. He had awarded Bruce the prize that gave the dog his championship. And now he must discrown this collie he loved. For the first time he must pass Bruce over and give winners to another and younger dog. Youth will be served! His heart as sore as an ulcer, his pale and half-shut eyes smarting, the hot and impotent wrath of old age boiling in his brain, Angus McGilead continued his meaningless and seemingly bored inspection of the two dogs.

He loved Bruce—better than ever before he had realised. He had always felt himself the marvellous collie's sponsor. And now—

Oh, why hadn't the dog's fool of an owner had sense enough to retire him from the ring before this inevitable downfall had come; this fate that lies craftily in wait for dog and horse and man who stay in the game too long?

The Master had said this was to be the old dog's last show. His last show! And he must leave the ring—-beaten! Beaten by a youngster, at that! A pup who had years and years of triumphs ahead of him. Surely the smugly perfect little tike could have waited till his sire's retirement, before beginning his own career of conquest! He needn't have started out by annexing dear old Bruce's scalp and by smashing the old dog's long record of victories!

Bruce! Glorious old Brucie, whose progress had been McGilead's own life-monument! To slink out of the ring—at his very last show, too—defeated by a puppy! Oh, this rotten cult of youth—youth—youth! He and Bruce were both back numbers at last.

But were they?

Bruce, bored by the long wait, nudged the Scotchman's inert fist with his cold nose, and sought to shake hands. This diversion brought the judge back to earth.

A gust of red rage set McGilead's blood to swirling. On fierce impulse he straightened his bent figure and unveiled his sleepy-looking eyes in a glare of fury.

He laid both hands on the head of the gallant old dog whom he idolised.

"Bruce wins!" he proclaimed, his rasping voice as harsh as a file on rusty iron. "Bruce wins!"

Wheeling on the Master, he croaked, in that same strained, rasping shout, the scrap of a schooldays' quotation which had come often to his memory of late.

"'It's safer playing with the lion's whelp than with the old lion dying!'" he mouthed. "Bruce wins! Retire him, now! 'Youth will be served.' But not till us oldsters are out of the way. Clear the ring!"

As he stamped from the enclosure he was buttonholed by a sporty-looking man whom he had met at many a show.

"Mr. McGilead," began the man, respectfully, "the Collie Club of the Union has appointed me a committee of one to engage you for judge at our annual show in November. Some of the members suggested a younger man. But the Old Guard held out for you. I was going to write, but—"

"It'd have done you no good!" growled McGilead, sick with shame. "Let me alone!"

"If it's a question of price—" urged the puzzled man.

"Price?" snarled McGilead, turning on him in senile fury. "Price? There's only one price. And I've paid it. I won't judge at your show! I'll never judge again at any show! My judging days are over! I'm a dead one! I'm an old, old man, I tell you! I'm in my dotage! I—why, I couldn't even trust myself, any more, to judge squarely. I'm through!"

SIX

Lochinvar Bobby

When the first Angus Mackellar left his ancestral Lochbuy moors he brought to America the big, shaggy, broad-headed collie dog he loved—the dog that had helped him herd his employer's sheep for the past five years.

Man and dog landed at Castle Garden a half century ago. From that time on, as for three hundred years earlier, no member of the Mackellar family was without a collie; the best and wisest to be found.

Evolution narrowed the heads and lightened the stocky frames of these collies, as the decades crawled past.

Evolution changed the successive generations of Mackellars not at all, except to rub smoother their Highland burr and to make them serve America as ardently as ever their forefathers had served Scotland. But not one of them lost his hereditary love for the dog of the moors.

Which brings us by degrees to Jamie Mackellar, grandson of the emigrating Angus. Jamie was twenty-eight. His tough little body was so meagrely spare that his big heart and bigger soul were almost indecently exposed. For the rest, his speech still held an occasional word or two of handed-down ancestral dialect. In moments of excitement these inherited phrases came thicker; and with them a tang of Scots accent.

Jamie lived in the cheapest suburb of Midwestburg, and in one of the suburb's cheapest houses. But the house had a yard. And the yard harboured a glorious old collie, a rare prize winner in his day. The house in front of the yard, by the way, harboured Jamie's Yorkshire wife and their two children, Elspeth and Donald.

Jamie divided his home time between the house and the open. So—after true Highland fashion—did the collie.

There were long rambles in the forests and the wild half-cleared land beyond the suburb; walks that meant as much to Jamie as to the dog, after the Scot had been driving a contractor's truck six days of the week for a monthly wage of seventy-five dollars.

Now, on seventy-five dollars a month many a family lives in comfort. But the sum leaves scant margin for the less practical luxuries of life. And in a sheepless and law-abiding region a high-quality collie is a nonpractical luxury. Yet Jamie would almost as soon have thought of selling one of his thick-legged children as of accepting any of the several good offers made him for the beautiful dog which had been his chum for so many years, the dog whose prize ribbons and cups from a score of local shows made gay the trophy corner of the Mackellar kitchen-parlour.

Then, on a late afternoon,—when the grand old collie was galloping delightedly across the street to meet his home-returning master,—a delivery motor car, driven by a speed-drunk boy, whizzed around the corner on the wrong side of the way.

The big dog died as he had lived—gallantly and without a whine. Gathering himself up from the muck of the road he walked steadfastly forward to meet the fast-running Mackellar. As Jamie bent down to search the mired body for injuries, the collie licked his master's dear hand, shivered slightly and fell limp across the man's feet.

When the magistrate next morning heard that a mouth-foaming little Scot had sprung upon the running board of a delivery car and had hauled therefrom a youth of twice his size and had hammered the said youth into 100 per cent. eligibility for a hospital cot, he listened gravely to the other side of the story and merely fined Jamie one dollar.

The released prisoner returned with bent head and barked knuckles to a house which all at once had been left unto him desolate. For the first time in centuries a Mackellar was without a collie.

During the next week the Midwestburg Kennel Association's annual dog show was held at the Fourth Regiment Armory. This show was one of the banner events of the year throughout Western dog circles. Its rich cash specials and its prestige even drew breeders from the Atlantic States to exhibit thereat the best their kennels afforded.

Thither, still hot and sore of heart, fared Jamie Mackellar. Always during the three days of the Midwestburg dog show Jamie took a triple holiday and haunted the collie section and the ringside. Here more than once his dead chum had won blue ribbon and cash over the exhibits from larger and richer kennels. And at such times Jamie Mackellar had rejoiced with a joy that was too big for words, and which could express itself only in a furtive hug of his collie's shaggy ruff.

To-day, as usual, Jamie entered the barnlike armory among the very first handful of spectators. To his ears the reverberant clangour of a thousand barks was as battle music; as it echoed from the girdered roof and yammered incessantly on the eardrums.

As ever, he made his way at once to the collie section. A famous New York judge was to pass upon this breed. And there was a turnout of nearly sixty collies; including no less than five from the East. Four of these came from New Jersey; which breeds more high-class collies than do any three other states in the Union.

It was Jamie's rule to stroll through the whole section, for a casual glance over the collies, before stopping at any of the benches for a closer appraisal. But to-day he came to a halt, before he had traversed the first row of stalls. His pale-blue eyes were riveted on a single dog.

Lying at lazily majestic ease on the straw of a double-size bench was a huge dark-sable collie. Full twenty-six inches high at the shoulder and weighing perhaps seventy-five pounds, this dog gave no hint of coarseness or of oversize. He was moulded as by a super-sculptor. His well-sprung ribs and mighty chest and leonine shoulders were fit complements to the classically exquisite yet splendidly strong head.

His tawny coat was as heavy as a bison's mane. The outer coat—save where it turned to spun silk, on the head—was harsh and wavy. The under coat was as impenetrably soft as the breast of an eider duck. From gladiator shoulders the gracefully powerful body sloped back to hips which spoke of lightning speed and endurance. The tulip ears had never known weights or pincers. The head was a true wedge, from every viewpoint. The deep-set dark eyes were unbelievably perfect in expression and placment.

Here was a collie! Here was a dog whose sheer perfection made Jamie Mackellar catch his breath for wonder, and then begin pawing frantically at his show catalogue. He read, half aloud:

729: Lochinvar Kennels. CHAMPION LOCHINVAR KING.
Lochinvar Peerless—Lochinvar Queen

Followed the birth date and the words "Breeder owner."

Jamie Mackellar's pale eyes opened yet wider and he stared on the collie with tenfold interest; an interest which held in it a splash of reverence. Jamie was a faithful reader of the dog press. And for the past two years Champion Lochinvar King's many pictures and infinitely more victories had stirred his admiration. He knew the dog, as a million Americans know Man-o'-War.

Now eagerly he scanned the wonder collie. Every detail,—from the level mouth and chiselled, wedge-shaped head and stern eyes with their true "look of eagles," to the fox brush tail with its sidewise swirl at the tip—Jamie scanned with the delight of an artist who comes for the first time on a Velasquez of which he has read and dreamed. Never in his dog-starred life had the little man beheld so perfect a collie. It was an education to him to study such a marvel.

Two more men came up to the bench. One was wearing a linen duster; and fell to grooming King's incredibly massive coat with expert hands. The other—a plump giant in exaggeratedly vivid clothes—chirped to the dog and ran careless fingers over the silken head. The collie waved his plumed tail in response to the caress. Recalling how coldly King had ignored his own friendly advances, Jamie Mackellar addressed the plump man in deep respect.

"Excuse me, sir," said he humbly, "but might you be Mr. Frayne—Mr. Lucius Frayne?"

The man turned with insolent laziness, eyed the shabby little figure from head to foot, and nodded. Then he went back to his inspection of King.

Not to be rebuffed, Mackellar continued:

"I remember reading about you when you started the Lochinvar Kennels, sir. That'll be—let's see—that'll be the best part of eight years ago. And three years back you showed Lochinvar Peerless out here—this great feller's sire. I'm proud to meet you, sir."

Frayne acknowledged this tribute by another nod, this time not even bothering to turn toward his admirer.

Mackellar pattered on:

"Peerless got Americanbred and Limit, that year; and he went to Reserve Winners. If I'd 'a' been judging, I'd of gave him Winners, over Rivers Pride, that topped him. Pride was a good inch-and-a-half too short in the brush. And the sable grew away too far from his eyes. Gave 'em a roundish, big look. He was just a wee peckle overshot too. And your Peerless outshowed him, besides. But, good as Peerless was, he wasn't a patch on this son of his you've got here to-day. Losh, but it sure looks like you was due to make a killing, Mr. Frayne."

And now the Eastern breeder deigned to face the man whose words were pattering so meekly into his heedless ears. Frayne realised this little chap was not one of the ignorant bores who pester exhibitors at every big show; but that he spoke, and spoke well, the language of the initiate. No breeder is above catering to intelligent praise of his dog. And Frayne warmed mildly toward the devotee.

"Like him, do you?" he asked, indulgently.

"Like him?" echoed Mackellar. "Like him? Man, he's fifty per cent the best I've set eyes on. And I've seen a hantle of 'em."

"Take him down, Roke," Frayne bade his linen-dustered kennel man. "Let him move about a bit. You can get a real idea of him when you see his action," he continued to the dazzled Mackellar. "How about that? Hey?"

At the unfastening of his chain, Lochinvar King stepped majestically to the floor and for an instant stood gazing up at his master. He stood as might an idealised statue of a collie. Mackellar caught his breath and stared. Then with expert eyes he watched the dog's perfect action as the kennel man led him up and down for half a dozen steps.

"He's—he's better even than I thought he could be," sighed Jamie. "He looked too good to be true. Lord, it does tickle a man's heartstrings to see such a dog! I—I lost a mighty fine collie a few days back," he went on confidingly. "Not in King's class, of course, sir. But a grand old dog. And—and he was my chum, too. I'm fair sick with greeting over him. It kind of crumples a feller, don't it, to lose a chum collie? One reason I wanted to come here early to-day was to look around and see were any of the for-sale ones inside my means. I've never been without a collie before. And I want to get me one—a reg'lar first-rater, like the old dog—as quick as I can. It's lonesome-like not to have a collie laying at my feet, evening times; or running out to meet me."

Lucius Frayne listened now with real interest to the little man's timid plaint.

As Mackellar paused, shamefaced at his own non-Scottish show of feeling, the owner of the Lochinvar Kennels asked suavely:

"What were you counting on paying for a new dog? Or hadn't you made up your mind?"

"Once in a blue moon," replied Mackellar, "a pretty good one is for sale cheap. Either before the judging or if the judge don't happen to fancy his type. I—well, if I had to, I was willing to spend a hundred—if I could get the right dog. But I tholed maybe I could get one for less."

Still more interestedly did Frayne beam down on the earnest little Mackellar.

"It's a pity you can't go higher," said he with elaborate nonconcern. "Especially since King here has caught your fancy. You see, I've got a four-month pup of King's, back home. Out of my winning Lochinvar Lassie, at that. I sold all the other six in the litter. Sold 'em at gilt-edge prices; on account of their breeding. This little four-monther I'm speaking about—he was so much the best of the lot that I was planning to keep him. He's the dead image of what King was at his age. He's got 'future champion' written all over him. But—well, since you've lost your chum dog and since you know enough of collies to treat him right—well, if you were back East

91

where you could look him over, I'd—well, I'd listen to your offer for him."

He turned toward his kennel man as if ending the talk. Like a well-oiled phonograph, the linen dustered functionary spoke up.

"Oh, Mr. Frayne!" he blithered, ceasing to groom King's wondrous coat and clasping both dirty hands together. "You wouldn't ever go and sell the little 'un? Not Lochinvar Bobby, sir? Not the best pup we ever bred? Why, he's 20 per cent. better than what King, here, was at his age. You'll make a champion of him by the time he's ten months old. Just like Doc Burrows did with his Queen Betty. He's a second Howgill Rival, that pup is;—a second Sunnybank Sigurd! You sure wouldn't go selling him? Not Bobby?"

"There'll be other Lochinvar King pups along in a few weeks, Roke," argued Frayne conciliatingly. "And this man has just lost his only dog. If—What a pair of fools we are!" he broke off, laughing loudly. "Here we go gabbling about selling Bobby, and our friend, here, isn't willing to go above a hundred dollars for a dog!"

The kennel man, visibly relieved, resumed operations on King with dandy-brush and cloth. But Mackellar stood looking up at Frayne as a hungry pup might plead dumbly with some human who had just taken from him his dinner bone.

"If—if he's due to be a second Lochinvar King," faltered Jamie, "I—I s'pose he'd be way beyond me. I'm a truck driver, you see, sir. And I've got a wife and a couple of kids. So I wouldn't have any right to spend too much, just for a dog—even if I had the cash. But—gee, but it's a chance!"

Sighing softly in renunciation, he took another long and admiring gaze at the glorious Lochinvar King; and then made as though to move away. But Lucius Frayne's dog-loving heart evidently was touched by Jamie's admiration for the champion and by the hinted tale of his chum dog's death. He stopped the sadly departing Mackellar.

"Tell me more about that collie you lost," he urged. "How'd he die? What was his breeding? Ever show him?"

Now perhaps there breathes some collie man who can resist one of those three questions about his favourite dog. Assuredly none lives who can resist all three. Mackellar, in a brace of seconds, found himself prattling eagerly to this sympathetic giant; telling of his dog's points and wisdom and lovableness, and of the prizes he had won; and, last of all, the tale of his ending.

Frayne listened avidly, nodding his head and grunting consolation from time to time. At last he burst forth, on impulse:

"Look here! You know dogs. You know collies. I see that. I'd rather have a Lochinvar pup go to a man who can appreciate him, as

92

you would, and who'd give him the sort of home you'd give him, than to sell him for three times as much, to some mucker. I'm in this game for love of the breed, not to skin my neighbours. Lochinvar Bobby is yours, friend, for a hundred and fifty dollars. I hope you'll say no," he added with his loud laugh, "because I'd rather part with one of my back teeth. But anyhow I feel decenter for making the offer."

Pop-eyed and scarlet and breathing fast, Jamie Mackellar did some mental arithmetic. One hundred and fifty dollars was a breath-taking sum. Nobody knew it better than did he. But—oh, there stood Lochinvar King! And King's best pup could be Jamie's for that amount.

Then Mackellar bethought him of an extra job that was afloat just now in Midwestburg—a job at trucking explosives by night from the tesladite factory, over on the heights, to the railroad. It was a job few people cared for. The roads were joggly. And tesladite was a ticklish explosive. Even the company's offer of fifty dollars a week, at short hours, had not brought forth many volunteer chauffeurs.

Yet Jamie was a careful driver. He knew he could minimise the risk. And by working three hours a night for three weeks he could clean up the price of the wonderful pup without going down into the family's slim funds.

"You're—you're on!" he babbled, shaking all over with pure happiness. "In three weeks I'll send you a money order. Here's—here's—let's see—here's twenty-seven dollars to bind the bargain."

"Roke," said Frayne, ignoring his kennel man's almost weeping protests, "scribble out a bill of sale for Lochinvar Bobby. And see he's shipped here the day we get this gentleman's money order for the balance of $150. And don't forget to send him Bobby's papers at the same time. Seeing it's such a golden bargain for him, he'll not grudge paying the expressage, too. I suppose I'm a wall-eyed fool, but—say! Hasn't a man got to do a generous action once in a while? Besides, it's all for the good of the breed."

Ten minutes later Mackellar tore away his ardent eyes from inspection of the grand dog whose best pup he was so soon to earn, and pattered on down the collie section.

Then and then only did Lucius Frayne and Roke look at each other. Long and earnestly they looked. And Frayne reached out his thick hand and shook his kennel man's soiled fingers. He shook them with much heartiness. He was a democratic sportsman, this owner of the famed Lochinvar Kennels. He did not disdain to grasp the toil-hardened hand of his honest servitor; especially at a time like this.

93

Lochinvar King that day clove his path straight through "Open, Sable-and-White" and "Open, any Colour," to "Winners"; in a division of fifty-eight collies. Then be annexed the cup and the forty dollars in cash awards for Best of Breed; also four other cash specials. And in the classic special for Best Dog in Show he came as near to winning as ever a present-day collie can hope to at so large a show. Jamie Mackellar, with a vibrating pride and a sense of personal importance, watched and applauded every win of his pup's matchless sire.

"In another year," he mused raptly, "I'll be scooping up them same specials with King's gorgeous little son. This man Frayne is sure one of the fellers that God made."

Four weeks and two days later, a past-worthy slatted crate, labelled "Lochinvar Collie Kennels," was delivered at Jamie's door. It arrived a bare ten minutes after Mackellar came home from work. All the family gathered around it in the kitchen; while, with hands that would not stay steady, the head of the house proceeded to unfasten the clamps which held down its top.

It was Jamie Mackellar' s great moment, and his wife and children were infected almost to hysteria by his long-sustained excitement.

Back went the crate lid. Out onto the kitchen floor shambled a dog.

For a long minute, as the new-arrived collie stood blinking and trembling in the light, everybody peered at him without word or motion. Jamie's jaw had gone slack, at first sight of him. And it still hung supine; making the man's mouth look like a frog penny bank's.

The puppy was undersized. He was scrawny and angular and all but shapeless. At a glance, he might have belonged to any breed or to many breeds or to none. His coat was sparse and short and kinky; and through it glared patches of lately-healed eczema. The coat's colour was indeterminate, what there was of it. Nor had four days in a tight crate improved its looks.

The puppy's chest was pitifully narrow. The sprawly legs were out at elbow and cow-hocked. The shoulders were noteworthy by the absence of any visible sign of them. The brush was an almost hairless rat-tail. The spine was sagged and slightly awry.

But the head was the most direful part of the newcomer. Its expressionless eyes were sore and dull. Its ears hung limp as a setter's. The nose and foreface were as snubbily broad as a Saint Bernard's. The slack jaw was badly overshot. The jowls showed a marked tendency to cheekiness and the skull seemed to be developing an apple-shaped dome in place of the semi-platform which the top of a collie's head ought to present.

Breed dogs as carefully and as scientifically as you will; once in a way some such specimen will be born into even the most blue-blooded litter;—a specimen whose looks defy all laws of clean heredity; a specimen which it would be gross flattery to call a mutt.

One of three courses at such times can be followed by the luckless breeder: To kill the unfortunate misfit; to give it away to some child who may or may not maul it to death; or to swindle a buyer into paying a respectable price for it.

Thriftily, Lucius Frayne had chosen the third course. And no law could touch him for the deal. He had played as safe, in his dirty trade, as does any vivisector.

Mackellar had bought the dog, sight unseen. Frayne had guaranteed nothing save the pedigree, which was flawless. He had said the creature was the image of King at the same age. But he had said it in the presence of no witness save his own kennel man. And the statement, in any event, was hard of refutal by law.

No; Frayne, like many another shrewd professional dog breeder, had played safe. And he had annexed one hundred and fifty dollars, in peril-earned hoardings, for a beast whose true cash value was less than eight cents to any one. He had not even bothered to give the cur a high-sounding pedigree name.

There stood, or crouched, the trembling and whimpering wisp of worthlessness; while the Mackellar family looked on in dumb horror. To add to the pup's ludicrous aspect, an enormous collar hung dangling from his neck. Frayne had been thrifty, in even this minor detail. Following the letter of the transportation rules, he had "equipped the dog with suitable collar and chain." But the chain, which Jamie had unclasped in releasing the pup from the crate, had been a thing of rust and flimsiness. The collar had been outworn by some grown dog. To keep it from slipping off over the puppy's head Roke had fastened to it a twist of wire, whose other end was enmeshed in the scattering short hairs of the youngster's neck. From this collar's ring still swung the last year's license tag of its former wearer.

It was little Elspeth who broke the awful spell of silence.

"Looks—looks kind of—of measly, don't he?" she volunteered.

"Jamie Mackellar!" shrilled her mother, finding voice and wrath in one swift gasp. "You—you went and gambled with your life on them explosion trucks—and never told me a word about it till it was over—just to earn money to buy—to buy—that!"

Then Jamie spoke. And at his first luridly sputtered sentence his wife shooed the children out of the room in scandalised haste. But from the cottage's farthest end she could hear her spouse's light voice still raised to shrill falsetto. He seemed to be in earnest converse with his Maker, and the absence of his wife and children from the room lent lustre and scope to his vocabulary.

Outside, the night was settling down bitterly chill. A drifting snow was sifting over the frozen earth. The winter's worst cold spell was beginning. But in the firelit kitchen a hope-blasted and swindled man was gripped by a boiling rage that all the frigid outer world could not have cooled.

Presently, through his sputtering soliloquy, Mackellar found time and justice to note that Lochinvar Bobby was still shaking with the cold of his long wagon ride through the snow from the station. And sullenly the man went out to the refrigerator in the back areaway for milk to warm for the sufferer.

He left the door open behind him. Into the kitchen seeped the deadly chill of night. It struck the miserable Bobby and roused him from the apathy of fright into which his advent to the bright room had immersed him.

The fright remained, but the impotence to move was gone. Fear had been born in his cringing soul, from the harsh treatment meted out to him in the place of his birth by kennel men who scoffed at his worthlessness. Fear had increased fifty fold by his long and clangorous journey across half the continent. Now, fear came to a climax.

He had cowered in helpless terror before these strangers, here in the closed room. He had sensed their hostility. But now for an instant the strangers had left him. Yes, and the back door was standing ajar—the door to possible escape from the unknown dangers which beset him on all sides.

Tucking his ratlike tail between his cow-hocks, Bobby put down his head and bolted. Through the doorway he scurried, dodging behind the legs of Jamie Mackellar as he fled through the refrigerator-blocked areaway. Jamie heard the scrambling footfalls, and turned in time to make a belated grab for the fleeing dog.

He missed Bobby by an inch; and the man's gesture seemed to the pup a new menace. Thus had Roke and the other kennel men struck at him in early days; or had seized him by tail or hind leg as he fled in terror from their beatings.

Out into the unfenced yard galloped the panic-driven Bobby. And through the pitch blackness Mackellar stumbled in utterly futile pursuit. The sound of Jamie's following feet lent new speed to the cowed youngster. Instead of stopping, after a few moments, he galloped on, with his ridiculous wavering and sidewise gait.

Mackellar lived on the outskirts of the suburb, which, in turn, was on the outskirts of the city. By chance or by instinct Bobby struck ahead for the rocky ridge which divided denser civilisation from the uncleared wilderness and the patches of farm country to the north. Nor did the puppy cease to run until he had topped, puffingly, the ridge's summit. There he came to a shambling halt and peered fearfully around him.

On the ridge-crest, the wind was blowing with razor sharpness. It cut like a billion waxed whiplashes, through the sparse coat and against the sagging ribs of the pup. It drove the snow needles into his watering eyes, and it stung the blown-back insides of his sensitive ears. He cowered under its pitiless might, as under a thrashing; and again he began to whimper and to sob.

Below him, from the direction whence he had wormed his slippery way up the ridge, lay the squalidly flat bit of plain with its sprinkle of mean houses; behind it, the straggling suburb whence he had escaped; and behind that, the far-reaching tangle of glare and blackness which was Midwestburg, with miles of lurid light reflection on the low-hanging clouds.

Turning, the puppy looked down the farther slope of his ridge to the rolling miles of forest and clearing, with wide-scattered farmsteads and cottages. The wilds seemed less actively and noisily terrifying than the glare and muffled roar of the city behind him. And, as anything was better than to cower freezing there in the wind's full path, Bobby slunk down the ridge's northern flank and toward the naked black woodlands beyond its base.

The rock edges and the ice cut his uncalloused splay feet. Even out of the wind, the chill gnawed through coat and skin. The world was a miserable place to do one's living in. Moreover, Bobby had not eaten in more than twenty-four hours; although a pup of his age is supposed to be fed not less than four times a day.

The rock-strewn ridge having been passed, the going became easier. Here, on the more level ground, a snow carpet made it softer, if colder. No longer running, but at a loose-jointed wolf trot, Bobby entered the woods. A quarter mile farther on, he stopped again; at sight of something which loomed up at a height of perhaps three feet above the half-acre of cleared ground about it.

He had strayed into the once-popular Blake's Woods Picnic Grove, and the thing which arrested his sick glance was the dancing platform which had been erected at the grove's painfully geometrical centre.

Years agone, Blake's Woods had been a favourite outing ground for Midwestburg's workers. The coming of the interurban trolley, which brought Boone Lake Beach within half an hour of the city, had turned these woods into a dead loss as far as local pleasure seekers were concerned. The benches had been split up or stolen or had rotted. The trim central patch of green sward had been left to grow successive unmown harvests of ragweed.

The dancing platform, with its once-smooth floor and the bright-painted lattice which ran around its base, was sharing the fate of the rest of the grove. The floor was sunken and holey. The laths of the lattice had fallen away in one or two places, and everywhere they had been washed free of their former gay paint.

Bobby's aimless course took him past one end of the platform, as soon as he discovered it was harmless and deserted. A furtive sidelong glance, midway of the latticed stretch, showed him a weed-masked hole some two feet square, where the laths had been ripped away or had been kicked in. The sight awoke vague submemories, centuries old, in the artificially reared pup. Thus had his wolf forbears seen, and explored for den purposes, gaps between rocks or under windfalls. Bobby, moving with scared caution, crept up to the opening, sniffed its musty interior; and, step by step, ventured in under the platform.

Here it was still bitter cold; yet it was sensibly warmer than in the open. And, year after year, dead leaves had been wind-drifted through the gap. Riffles of them lay ankle deep near the entrance. Down into the thickest of the riffles the wretched puppy wiggled his shivering way. There he lay, still shaking, but gaining what scant comfort he might from the warmth of the leaves beneath and around him.

Presently from sheer nervous fatigue he snoozed.

It was past midnight when Bobby awoke. He was awakened less by cold than by ravening hunger. His was not the normal increase of appetite that had come upon him at such times as the Lochinvar kennel men had been an hour or so late with his dinner. This was the first phase of famine.

Fear and discomfort had robbed him of hunger throughout the train journey. But now he was safe away from the strangers who had seemed to menace his every move; and he had had a few hours of sleep to knit his frayed nerves. He was more than hungry. He was famished. All his nature cried out for food.

Now, never in his brief life had Lochinvar Bobby found his own meals. Never had he so much as caught a mouse or rifled a garbage pail. In sanitary man-made kennel run and hutch had he passed all his time. Not his had been the human companionship which sharpens a collie's brain as much as does stark need. And he had no experience of food, save that which had been served him in a

98

tin dish. He did not know that food grows in any other form or place.

But here was no tin dish heaped with scientifically balanced, if uninspired, rations. Here was no manner of food at all. Bobby nosed about among the dead leaves and the mould of his new-found den. Nothing was there which his sense of smell recognised as edible. And goaded by the scourge of hunger he ventured out again into the night. The wind had dropped. But the cold had only intensified; and a light snow was still sifting down.

Bobby stood and sniffed. Far off, his sensitive nostrils told him, was human habitation. Presumably that meant food was there, too. Humans and food, in Bobby's experience, always went together. The pup followed the command of his scent and trotted dubiously toward the distant man-reek.

In another quarter-hour the starving pup was sniffing about the locked kitchen door of a farmhouse. Within, he could smell milk and meat and bread. But that was all the good it did him. Timidly he skirted the house for ingress. Almost had he completed the round when a stronger odour smote his senses. It was a smell which, of old he would have disregarded. But, with the primal impulse of famine, other atavistic traits were stirring in the back of his necessity-sharpened brain.

His new scent was not of prepared food, but of hot and living prey. Bobby paused by the unlatched door of the farm chicken coop. Tentatively he scratched at the white-washed panel. Under the pressure the door swung inward. Out gushed a pleasant warmth and a monstrously augmented repetition of the whiff which had drawn him to the henhouse.

Just above him, well within reach, perched fifteen or twenty feathery balls of varicoloured fluff. And famine did the rest.

Acting on some impulse wholly beyond his ken, Bobby sprang aloft and drove his white milk teeth deep into the breast of a Plymouth Rock hen.

Instantly, his ears were assailed by a most ungodly racket. The quiet hencoop was hideous with eldritch squawks and was alive with feathers. All Bobby's natural fear urged him to drop this flapping and squawking hen and to run for his life.

But something infinitely more potent than fear had taken hold upon him. Through his fright surged a sensation of mad rapture. He had set teeth in live prey. Blood was hot in his nostrils. Quivering flesh was twisting and struggling between his tense jaws. For the moment he was a primitive forest beast.

Still gripping his noisy five-pound burden, he galloped out of

99

the hencoop and across the barnyard; heading instinctively for the lair in which he had found a soft bed and safety from human intruders. As he fled, he heard a man's bellowing voice. A light showed in an upper window of the house. Bobby ran the faster.

The hen was heavy, for so spindling a killer. But Bobby's overshot jaws held firm. He dared not pause to eat his kill, until he should be safe away from the shouting man.

Stumbling into his platform den, half dead with hunger and fatigue, the dog sought his bed of leaves. And there he feasted, rather than ate. For never before had he known such a meal. And when the last edible morsel of it was gorged, he snuggled happily down in his nest and slept.

Poultry bones are the worst and most dangerous fare for any domesticated dog. Their slivers tear murderously at throat and stomach and intestines; and have claimed their slain victims by the hundred. Yet, since the beginning of time, wild animals, as foxes and wolves, have fed with impunity on such bones. No naturalist knows just why. And for some reason Bobby was no more the worse for his orgy of crunched chicken-bones than a coyote would have been.

He awoke, late in the morning. Some newborn sense, in addition to his normal fear, warned him to stay in his den throughout the daylight hours. And he did so; sleeping part of the time and part of the time nosing about amid the flurry of feathers in vain search for some overlooked bone or fragment of meat.

Dusk and hunger drove him forth again. And, as before, he sought the farmstead which had furnished him with so delicious a meal. But as he drew near, the sound of voices from indoors and the passing of an occasional silhouette across the bright window shades of the kitchen warned him of danger.

When, as the kitchen light was blown out, he ventured to the chicken coop he found the door too fast-barred to yield to his hardest scratch. Miserably hungry and disappointed he slunk away.

Three farms did Bobby visit that night before he found another with an unlatched henhouse door. There the tragedy of the preceding evening was repeated. Lugging an eight-pound Dominic rooster, Bobby made scramblingly for his mile-distant lair. Behind him again raged sound and fury. The eight-pound bird with its dangling legs and tail feathers kept tripping up the fleeing dog; until, acting again on instinct, Bobby slung the swaying body over his shoulder, fox-fashion, and thus made his way with less discomfort.

By the third night the collie had taken another long step in his journey backward to the wild. When a dog kills a chicken every one within a half mile is likely to be drawn by the sound. When a fox or wolf or coyote kills a chicken, the deed is done in dexterous silence; with no squawks or flurry of feathers to tell the story. Nature teaches the killer this secret. And Nature taught it to Bobby; as she has taught it to other gone-wild dogs.

As a result, his depredations, thereafter, left no uproar behind them. Also, he learned presently the vulpine art of hoarding;—in other words, when safety permitted, to stay on the ground until he had not only slain but eaten one chicken, and then to carry another bird back to his lair for future use. It cut down the peril of over-many trips to neighbouring coops.

In time, he learned to rely less and less on the close-guarded chickens in the vicinity of his den, and to quarter the farm country for a radius of ten or more miles in search of food. The same queer new instinct taught him infinite craft in keeping away from humans and in covering his tracks.

He was doing no more than are thousands of foxes throughout the world. There was no miracle in his new-found deftness as a forager. Nature was merely telling her ancient and simple secrets to a wise little brain no longer too clogged by association with mankind to learn them.

There was a profitable side line to Bobby's chicken hunts. The wilder woods, back of Midwestburg, abounded in rabbits for such as had the wit to find them. And Bobby acquired the wit.

Incredibly soon, he learned the wolf's art of tracking a cottontail and of stalking the prey until such moment as a lightning dash and a blood-streaked swirl in the snow marked the end of the chase. Squirrels, too, and an occasional unwary partridge or smaller bird, were added to the collie's menu. And more than once, as he grew stronger, Bobby lugged homeward over his shoulder a twenty-pound lamb from some distant sheepfold.

Nature had played a vilely cruel trick on Lochinvar Bobby by bringing him into the world as the puny and defective runt of a royal litter. She had threatened his life by casting him loose in the winter woods. But at that point Nature seemed to repent of her unkindness to the poor helpless atom of colliehood. For she taught him the closest-guarded secrets of her awful Live-On-One-Another ritual.

As winter grew soggy at the far approach of spring, Bobby found less and less trouble in making a nightly run of thirty miles in search of meals or in carrying back to his lair the heaviest of burdens.

Feasting on raw meat—and plenty of it—living in the open,

101

with the icy cold for his bedfellow, he was taking one of the only two courses left to those who must forage or die. Readily enough he might have dwindled and starved. The chill weather might have snuffed out his gangling life. Instead, the cold and the exposure, and the needful exercise, and the life according to forest nature, and the rich supply of meat that was his for the catching—all these had worked wonders on the spindling runt.

His narrow chest had filled out, from much lung work. His shoulders, from the same cause and from incessant night running, had taken on a splendid breadth. His gawkily shambling body grew rapidly. The overshot puppy jaw was levelling. And as his frame grew it shaped itself along lines of powerful grace, such as Nature gives to the leopard and to the stag. Incessant exposure to the cold had changed his sparse covering of hair to a coat whose thickness and length and texture would have been the wonder of the dog-show world. In brief, his mode of life was achieving for him what all the kennel experts and vets unhung could not have accomplished.

It had been a case of kill or cure. Bobby was cured.

After the departure of the snows and the zero nights, and before the leafage made secret progress safe through forest and meadow, Bobby knew a period of leanness. True, he foraged as before, but he did it at far greater risk and with less certainty of results.

For—he could not guess why—the countryside was infested nowadays with armed men; men who carried rifle or shot-gun and who not only scoured hill and valley by daylight but lurked outside chicken coops and sheepfolds by night.

Of course, by day Bobby could avoid them—and he did—by lying close in his den. And at night his amazingly keen sense of smell enabled him to skirt them, out of gun-shot range, as they waited at barn door or at fold gate. But such necessity for caution played havoc with his chances for easily acquired food. And for the most part he had to fall back on rabbit-catching or to travelling far afield. This, until the thickening of foliage made his hunting excursions safer from detection by human eye.

There was sufficient reason for all this patrolling of the district. During the past few months word had seeped through the farm country that a wolf was at large in the long wolfless region; and that he was slaughtering all manner of livestock, from pullets to newborn calves.

No dog, it was argued, could be the killer. For no known dog could slay so silently and cover his tracks with such consummate skill. Nor could a fox carry away a lamb of double its own weight.

The marauder must be a wolf. And old-timers raked up yarns of the superhumanly clever exploits of lone wolves, in the days when populous Midwestburg was a trading post.

The county Grange took up the matter and offered a bounty of fifty dollars for the wolf's scalp and ears. It was a slack time on the farms—the period between woodcutting and early planting. It was a slack time in Midwestburg, too; several mills having shut down for a couple of months.

Thus, farmers and operatives amused themselves by making a try for the fifty dollars and for the honour of potting the super-wolf. It was pleasant if profitless sport for the hunters. But it cut down Bobby's rations; until farm work and reopening mills called off the quest. Then life went on as before; after a buckshot graze on the hip had taught the collie to beware of spring guns and to know their scent.

So the fat summer drowsed along. And so autumn brought again to the northern air the tang which started afresh the splendid luxuriance of the tawny coat which Bobby had shed during the first weeks of spring.

Late in December the dog had a narrow escape from death. A farmer, furious at the demise of his best Jersey calf, went gunning afresh for the mysterious wolf. With him he took along a German police dog—this being before the days when that breed was de-Germanised into the new title of "shepherd dog." He had borrowed the police dog for the hunt, lured by its master's tales of his pet's invincible ferocity.

Man and dog had searched the woods in vain all day, some five miles to north of Bobby's cave. At early dusk they were heading homeward through a rock gulch.

The wind was setting strong from the north. Midway through the gulch the police dog halted, back abristle, growling far down in his throat. The man looked up.

As he did so, Bobby topped the cliff which formed the gulch's northerly side. The collie was on his way to a farm in the valley beyond, which he had not visited for so long a time that its occupants might reasonably be supposed to have relaxed some of their unneighbourly vigilance. The wind from the north kept him from smelling or hearing the two in the gully a hundred feet to south of him.

Yet, reaching the summit, Bobby paused; his wonted caution bidding him search the lower grounds for sign of danger, before travelling farther by fading daylight in such an exposed position.

It was then that the farmer saw him clearly, for the best part of two seconds, silhouetted against the dying sunset. The man knew

103

little enough of collies, and less of wolves. And his mental vision was set for a wolf. Thus, to the best of his belief, a wolf was what he saw. But he saw also something he had not expected to see.

The last rays of the sun glinted on a bit of metal that swung beneath Bobby's shaggy throat; metal that had been worn bright by constant friction with the dog's ruff.

Thanks to the twist of wire which had been fastened into his hair, Bobby had not slipped the leathern collar wherewith Frayne had equipped him. And later his swelling muscular neck had been large enough to hold it on. From its ring the old license tag still dangled.

Up went the farmer's gun. He fired both barrels. As he pressed the two triggers at once, the police dog made a rush for the collie. The farmer chanced to be just in front of his canine companion. The police dog sought a short cut, to reach his foe, by diving between the marksman's slightly spread legs. The two gun barrels were fired straight upward into the sky; and the tripped-up hunter sat down with extreme suddenness on a pointed jut of rock.

By the time he could focus his maddened gaze on the cliff-top again, Bobby had vanished. The police dog was charging over the summit at express-train speed. The farmer shook an impotent fist after the disappearing spoiler of his aim.

"I hope he licks the life out of you if you ever catch up with him, you bunglin' fool!" he bellowed.

His wish came true. Next day, in a hollow, a mile farther on, the body of the police dog was found, a score of slashes on his greyish hide and one through his jugular. No police dog ever lived that could catch up with a galloping collie who did not want to be caught. Bobby had varied a career of profit with a moment or two of real pleasure.

Two days later, in the Midwestburg Herald, Jamie Mackellar read the account of this fragmentary drama. He scanned it with no deep interest. Tales of the wolf had grown stale to Herald readers. But suddenly his attention focused itself on the line:

"Mr. Gierson declares that a small disk of metal was suspended from the throat of the brute."

Jamie laid down the paper and went into executive session with his own inner consciousness. A disk of metal, suspended from the throat of an animal, means but one thing. It is a license tag. Never has such a tag been fastened to a wolf.

Back into Mackellar's memory came the picture of a poor shivering waif from whose meagre and almost naked throat hung a huge collar; a collar affixed by wire which was wound into such sparse strands of hair as could be made to support it.

On the morning after the next snowfall, Jamie took a day off. Carrying only a collar and chain and a muzzle, he fared forth into the woods. All day he hunted. He found nothing.

A week later came another snowfall in the night. Next morning Mackellar set forth again; this time letting his little son Donald come along. He had told his family the far-fetched suspicion that had dawned upon him, and Donald had clamoured to join the hunt.

On his first search, Jamie had quartered the country to west of the ridge. To-day he climbed the rocks and made his way into the rolling land below. Skirting Blake's Woods, he was moving on toward the farms when, in the fresh snow, he came upon the tracks he sought. For an hour he followed them. Apparently they led nowhere. At least, they doubled twice upon themselves and then vanished on a long outcrop of snowless rock which stretched back into Blake's Woods.

Tiring of this fruitless way of spending the morning, Donald strayed from his father. Into the woods he wandered. And presently he sighted the dancing platform amid its tangle of dead weeds. Running over to it, the boy climbed thereon. Then, striking an attitude, he began to harangue an invisible audience, from the platform edge; after the manner of a cart-tail political orator he had observed with emulous delight.

"My friends!" he shrilled, from memory, "Our anc'st'rs fit fer the lib'ty we enjoy! Are we goin' to—? Ouch! Hey, Daddy!"

One rhetorically stamping little foot had smashed through the rotten boarding. Nor could Donald draw it out. At the yell of fright, Jamie came running. But, a few yards from his son, Mackellar slid to a stop. His eyes were fixed on an opening just below the boy's imprisoned foot; an opening from which the passage of Donald's advancing body had cleared aside some of the tangled weeds. From the tip of a ragged lath, at the edge of this aperture, fluttered a tuft of tawny hair.

Pulling Donald free, Mackellar got down on all fours and peeped into the space beneath the platform. For a few seconds he could see nothing. Then, as his eyes accustomed themselves to the dimness, he descried two greenish points of light turned toward him from the farthest corner of the lair.

"Bobby?" called the man doubtfully.

The cornered dog heard the name. It roused vague half memories. The memories were not pleasant; though the voice had in it a friendliness that stirred the collie strangely.

Bobby crouched the closer to earth and his lips writhed back from murderous white teeth. The man called again; in the same

105

friendly, coaxing voice. Then he began to crawl forward a foot or so. Behind him the excited boy was blocking the only way out of the den.

The Lochinvar Bobby of ten months ago would have cowered whimperingly in his corner, waiting for capture. He might even have pleaded for mercy by rolling over on his back.

The Lochinvar Bobby of to-day was quite another creature. He laid out his plan of campaign, and then in the wink of an eye he carried it into effect.

With a rabid snarl he charged the advancing man. As Jamie braced himself to fend off the ravening jaws, the dog veered sharply to one side and dashed for the opening. Instinct told him the boy would be easier to break past than the man.

But it was not Jamie Mackellar's first experience with fighting or playing dogs. As Bobby veered, Jamie slewed his own prostrate body to the same side and made a grab for the fast-flying collie. His fingers closed and tightened around Bobby's left hind leg, just below the hock.

With a snarl, Bobby wheeled and drove his jaws at the captor's wrist; in a slash which might well have severed an artery. But, expecting just such a move, Jamie was ready with his free hand. Its fingers buried themselves in the avalanche of fur to one side of Bobby's throat. The slashing eye-teeth barely grazed the pinioning wrist. And Bobby thrashed furiously from side to side, to free himself and to rend his enemy.

Mackellar's expert hands found grips to either side of the whirling jaws, and he held on. Bit by bit, bracing himself with all his wiry strength, he backed out; dragging the frantic beast behind him.

Five minutes later, at the expense of a few half-averted bites, he had the muzzle tight-bound in place and was leading the exhausted and foaming collie toward Midwestburg. Bobby held back, he flung himself against the chain, he fought with futile madness against the gentle skill of his master.

Then shuddering all over he gave up the fight. Head and tail a-droop, he suffered himself to be led to prison.

"It's Lochinvar Bobby, all right!" the wondering Jamie was saying to his son in intervals of lavishing kindly talk and pats on the luckless dog. "The collar and tag prove that. But if it wasn't for them, I'd swear it couldn't be the same. It's—it's enough to take a body's breath away, Donald! I've followed the dog game from the time I was born, but I never set eyes on such a collie in all my days. Just run your hand through that coat! Was there ever another like it? And did you ever see such bone and head? He's—Lord, to think how he looked when that Frayne crook sawed him off on me! It's a miracle he lived through the first winter. I never heard of but one other case like it. And that happened up in Toronto, if I remember right.

"Now, listen, sonny: I'm not honing to be sued for damages by every farmer in the county. So let' em keep on looking for their wolf. This is a dog I bought last year. He's been away in the country till now. That's the truth. And the rest is nobody's business. But—but if it keeps me speiring for a week, to figger it out, I'm going to hit on some way to let Mr. Lucius Frayne, Esquire, see he hasn't stung me so hard as he thought he did!"

For two days Bobby refused to eat or drink. In the stout inclosure built for him in Mackellar's back yard he stood, head and tail a-droop, every now and then shivering as if with ague. Then, little by little, Jamie's skilled attentions did their work. The wondrous lure of human fellowship, the joy of cooked food, and the sense of security against harm, and, above all, a collie's ancestral love for the one man he chooses for his god—these wrought their work.

In less than a fortnight Bobby was once more a collie. The spirit of the wild beast had departed from him; and he took his rightful place as the chum of the soft-voiced little Scot he was learning to worship. Yes, and he was happy,—happier than ever before;—happy with a new and strangely sweet contentment. He had come into a collie's eternal heritage.

The Westminster Kennel Club's annual dog show at Madison Square Garden, in New York, is the foremost canine classic of America and, in late years, of the whole world.

A month before that year's Westminster Show, Lucius Frayne received a letter which made the wontedly saturnine sportsman laugh till the tears spattered down his nose. The joke was too good to keep to himself. So he shouted for Roke, and bade the kennel man share the fun of it with him.

He read aloud, cacklingly, to the listening Roke:

Mr. Lucius Frayne,
My dear Sir:

Last year, out to the Midwestburg show, here, you sold me a fine puppy of your Ch. Lochinvar King. And as soon as I could raise the price you sent him on here to me. I would of written to you when I got him, to thank you and to say how pleased I was with him and how all my friends praised him. But I figured you're a busy man and you

107

haven't got any waste time to spend in reading letters about how good your dogs are. Because you know it already. And so I didn't write to you. But I am writing to you now. Because this is business.

You know what a grand pup Bobby was when you sent him to me? Well to my way of thinking he has developed even better than he gave promise to. And some of my friends say the same. To my way of thinking he is the grandest collie in North America or anywhere else to-day. He is sure one grand dog. He turned out every bit as good as you said he would. He's better now than he was at five months.

I want to thank you for letting me have such a dog, Mr. Frayne. Just as you said, he is of Champion timber. Now this brings me to the business I spoke about.

Granther used to tell me how the gentry on the other side would bet with each other on their dogs at the shows. Six months ago my Aunt Marjorie died and she willed me nine hundred dollars ($900). It is in bank waiting for a good investment for it. Now here is an investment that seems to me a mighty safe one. Me knowing Bobby as I do. A fine sporting investment. And I hope it may please you as well. I am entering Bobby for Westminster. I read in Dog News that you are expecting to enter Champion Lochinvar King there, with others of your string. So here is my proposition.

I propose you enter King for "Open, Sable-and-White" and "Open, Any Colour," these being the only regular classes a sable champion is eligible for. I will enter Bobby in the same classes, instead of "Novice" as I was going to. And I will wager you six hundred dollars ($600) even, that the judge will place Bobby above King. I am making this offer knowing how fine King is but thinking my dog is even better. For Bobby has really improved since a pup. My wife thinks so too.

If this offer pleases you, will you deposit a certified check of six hundred dollars ($600) with the editor of Dog News? He is a square man as every one knows and he will see fair play. He has promised me he will hold the stakes. I am ready to deposit my certified check for six hundred dollars ($600) at once. I would like to bet the whole nine hundred dollars ($900). Knowing it a safe investment. Knowing Bobby like I do. But my wife doesn't want me to bet it at all and so we are compromising on six hundred dollars ($600).

Please let me hear from you on this, Mr. Frayne. And I thank you again for how you treated me as regards Bobby. I hope to repay you at Westminster by letting you see him for yourself.

Your ob't servant,
James A. Mackellar.

Yes, it was a long letter. Yet Frayne skipped no word of it. And Roke listened, as to heavenly music.

"Talk about Lochinvar luck!" chortled Frayne as he finished. "The worst pup we ever bred; and we sold him for one-fifty! And now he is due to fetch us another six hundred, in dividends. He—"

"You're going to cover his bet?" queried Roke. "Good! I was afraid maybe you'd feel kind of sorry for the poor cuss, and—"

"Unless I break both wrists, in the next hour," announced Frayne, "that certified check will start for the Dog News office by noon. It's the same old wheeze: A dub has picked up a smattering of dog talk; he thinks he knows it all. He buys a bum pup with a thundering pedigree. The pedigree makes him think the pup is a humdinger. He brags about it to his folks. They think anything that costs so much must be the best ever, no matter how it looks. And he gets to believing he's got a world beater. Then—"

"But, boss," put in Roke with happy unction, "just shut your eyes and try to remember how that poor mutt looked! And the boob says he's 'even better than he gave promise to be.' Do you get that? Yet you hear a lot about Scotchmen being shrewd! Gee, but I wish you'd let me have a slice of that $600 bet! I'd—"

"No," said Frayne judicially. "That's my own meat. It was caught in my trap. But I tell you what you can do: Wait till I send my check and till it's covered, and then write to Mackellar and ask him if he's willing to bet another $150, on the side, with you. From the way he sounds, you ought to have it easy in getting him to make the side bet. He needn't tell his wife. Try it anyhow; if you like."

Roke tried it. And, after ridiculously small objection on Jamie's part, the side bet was recorded and its checks were posted with the editor of Dog News. Once more Lucius Frayne and his faithful kennel man shook hands in perfect happiness.

To the topmost steel rafters, where the grey February shadows hung, old Madison Square Garden echoed and reverberated with the multi-keyed barks of some two thousand dogs. The four-day show had been opened at ten o'clock of a slushy Wednesday morning. And as usual the collies were to be judged on the first day.

109

Promptly at eleven o'clock the clean-cut collie judge followed his steward into the ring. The leather-lunged runner passed down the double ranks of collie benches, bawling the numbers for the Male Puppy Class.

The judge had a reputation for quickness, as well as for accuracy and honesty. The Open classes, for male dogs, were certain to come up for verdict within an hour, at most.

Seven benches had been thrown into one, for the Frayne dogs. At its back ran a strip of red silk, lettered in silver: "LOCHINVAR COLLIE KENNELS." Seven high-quality dogs lay or sat in this space de luxe. In the centre—his name on a bronze plate above his head—reclined Lochinvar King.

In full majesty of conscious perfection he lay there; magnificent as a Numidian lion, the target for all eyes. Conditioned and groomed to the minute, he stood out from his high-class kennel-mates like a swan among cygnets.

Frayne, more than once in the show's first hour or so, left his much-admired benches; for a glance at a near-by unoccupied space, numbered 568. Here, according to the catalogue, should be benched Lochinvar Bobby.

But Bobby was nowhere to be seen.

Congratulating himself on his own craft in having inserted a forfeit clause in the bet agreement, Frayne was none the less disappointed that the fifth-rate mutt had not shown up.

He longed for a chance to hear the titter of the railbirds; when the out-at-elbow, gangling, semi-hairless little nondescript should shamble into the ring. Bobby's presence would add zest to his own oft-told tale of the wager.

According to American Kennel Club rules, a dog must be on its bench from the moment the exhibition opens until the close, excepting only when it is in the ring or at stated exercise periods. That rule, until recently, has been most flagrantly disregarded by many exhibitors. In view of this, Frayne made a trip to the exercise room and then through the dim-lit stalls under the main floor.

As he came back from a fruitless search for Bobby or for Mackellar, he passed the collie ring. "Limit; Dogs," was chalked on the blackboard. Two classes more—"Open, Merle," and "Open, Tricolour"—and then King must enter the ring for "Open, Sable." Frayne hurried to the Lochinvar benches, where Roke and another kennel man were fast at work putting finishing touches to King's toilet.

The great dog was on his feet, tense and eager for the coming clash. Close behind the unseeing Roke, and studying King with grave admiration, stood Jamie Mackellar.

110

"Hello, there!" boomed Frayne with loud cordiality, bearing down upon the little man. "Get cold feet? I see your dog's absent. Remember, you forfeit by absence."

"Yes, sir," said Jamie with meekness, taking off his hat to the renowned sportsman, and too confused in fumbling with its wabbly brim to see the hand which Frayne held out to him. "Yes, sir. I remember the forfeit clause, sir. I'm not forfeiting. Bobby is here."

"Here? Where? I looked all over the—"

"I hired one of the cubby-hole rooms upstairs, sir; to keep him in, nights, while he's here. And I haven't brought him down to his bench yet. You see, he—he ain't seen many strangers. And you'll remember, maybe, that he used to be just a wee peckle shy. So I'm keeping him there till it is time to show him. My boy, Donald, is up, now, getting him ready. They'll be down presently, sir. I think you'll be real pleased with how Bobby looks."

"I'm counting on a heap of pleasure," was Frayne's cryptic reply, as he turned away to mask a grin of utter joy.

Five grey dogs were coming down the aisle to their benches. The Merle Class had been judged and the Tricolours were in the ring. There were but four of these.

In another handful of minutes the "Open, Sable" Class was called. It was the strongest class of the day. It contained no less than three champions; in addition to four less famous dogs, like Bobby;— seven entries in all.

Six of these dogs were marched into the ring. The judge looked at the steward, for the "all-here" signal. As he did so, the seventh entrant made his way past the gate crowd and was piloted into the ring by a small and cheaply clad man.

While the attendant was slipping the number board on Mackellar's arm, Lucius Frayne's eyes fell upon Lochinvar Bobby. So did those of the impatient judge and the ninety out of every hundred of the railbirds.

Through the close-packed ranks of onlookers ran a queer little wordless mutter—the most instinctive and therefore the highest praise that can be accorded.

Alertly calm of nerve, heedless of his surroundings so long as his worshipped god was crooning reassurances to him, Bobby stood at Mackellar's side.

His incredible coat was burnished like old bronze. His head was calmly erect, his mighty frame steady. His eyes, with true eagle look, surveyed the staring throng.

Never before, in all the Westminster Club's forty-odd shows, had such a collie been led into the ring. Eugenic breeding, wise

111

rationing and tireless human care had gone to the perfecting of other dogs. But Mother Nature herself had made Lochinvar Bobby what he was. She had fed him bountifully upon the all-strengthening ration of the primal beast; and she had given him the exercise-born appetite to eat and profit by it. Her pitiless winter winds had combed and winnowed his coat as could no mortal hand, giving it thickness and length and richness beyond belief. And she had moulded his growing young body into the peerless model of the Wild.

Then, because he had the loyal heart of a collie and not the incurable savagery of the wolf, she had awakened his soul and made him bask rapturously in the friendship of a true dog-man. The combination was unmatchable.

"Walk your dogs, please," ordered the judge, coming out of his momentary daze.

Before the end of the ring's first turn, he had motioned Frayne and Mackellar to take their dogs into one corner. He proceeded to study the five others; awarding to two of them the yellow third-prize ribbon and the white reserve, and then ordering the quintet from the ring. After which he beckoned Bobby and King to the judging block.

In the interim, Frayne had been staring goggle-eyed at the Midwestburg collie. He tried to speak; but he could not. A hundred thoughts were racing dumbly through his bemused brain. He stood agape, foolish of face.

Jamie Mackellar was pleasantly talkative.

"A grand class, this," he confided to his voiceless comrade. "But, first crack, Judge Breese had the eye to single out our two as so much the best that he won't size 'em up with the others. How do you like Bobby, sir? Is he very bad? Don't you think, maybe, he's picked up, just a trifle, since you shipped him to me? He's no worse, anyhow, than he was then, is he?"

Frayne gobbled, wordlessly.

"This is the last time I'll show him, for a while, Mr. Frayne," continued Jamie, a grasping note coming into his timid voice. "The cash I'm due to collect from you and Mr. Roke will make enough, with the legacy and what I've saved, to start me in business with a truck of my own. Bobby and I are going into partnership. And we're going to clean up. Bobby is putting seven hundred and fifty dollars and to-day's cash prizes into the firm. He and I are getting out of the show-end of collie breeding, for a time. The more we see of some of you professionals, the better we like cesspools. If dogs weren't the grandest animals the good Lord ever put on earth, a few of the folks

112

who exploit them would have killed the dog game long ago. It—. Judge Breese is beckoning for us!"

Side by side, the two glorious collies advanced to the judging block. Side by, side, at their handlers' gestures, they mounted it. And again from the railbirds arose that queer wordless hum. Sire and son, shoulder to shoulder, faced the judge.

And, for the first time in his unbroken career of conquest, Lochinvar King looked almost shabby; beside the wondrous young giant he had sired. His every good point—and he had no others—was bettered by Bobby.

As a matter of form, Breese went over both dogs with meticulous care; testing coat-texture, spring of ribs, action, soundness of bone, carriage, facial expression, and the myriad other details which go into the judging of a show dog. Long he faced them, crouching low and staring into their deep-set eyes; marking the set and carriage of the tulip ears; comparing point with point; as becomes a man who is about to give victory to an Unknown over a hitherto Invincible.

Then with a jerk of his head he summoned the steward with the judging book and ribbons. And, amid a spontaneous rattle of applause, Jamie Mackellar led his splendid dog to the far end of the ring, with one hand; while in the fingers of the other fluttered a strip of gold-lettered dark blue ribbon.

Back came both collies for the "Open, Any Colour Class," and the verdict was repeated; as it was repeated in the supreme "Winners'" Class which followed. "Winners'" Class carried, with its rosette and cash specials, a guerdon of five points toward Bobby's championship.

Then followed the rich harvest of other cash specials in the collie division, including $25 for "Best of Breed," and for the next three days even fatter gleanings from among the variety classes and unclassified specials. These last awards ranged from five dollars to twenty-five dollars apiece; apart from a valiseful of silver cups and like trophies which are more beautiful than pawnable.

On Saturday, Jamie Mackellar and Bobby took the midnight train for Midwestburg; richer by almost nine hundred dollars for their New York sojourn.

Rolling sweetly around in Jamie's memory was a brief talk he had had with Roke, an hour before the close of the show. Sent as emissary by Frayne, the kennel manager had offered Mackellar a flat two thousand dollars for the sensational young prize winner.

"We're not parting company, Bobby and I," Jamie had made civil answer. "Thanking you and your boss just as much. But tell Mr.

113

Frayne if ever I breed a pup as good as Bobby was when he came to me, he can have it for an even hundred and fifty. I wouldn't want such a fine chap to think I'm not just as clean a sportsman as what he is!"

SEVEN

"One Minute Longer"

Wolf was a collie, red-gold and white of coat, with a shape more like his long-ago wolf ancestors' than like a domesticated dog's. It was from this ancestral throw-back that he was named Wolf.

He looked not at all like his great sire, Sunnybank Lad, nor like his dainty, thoroughbred mother, Lady. Nor was he like them in any other way, except that he inherited old Lad's staunchly gallant spirit and loyalty and uncanny brain. No, in traits as well as in looks, he was more wolf than dog. He almost never barked, his snarl supplying all vocal needs.

The Mistress or the Master or the Boy—any of these three could romp with him, roll him over, tickle him, or subject him to all sorts of playful indignities. And Wolf entered gleefully into the fun of the romp. But let any human, besides these three, lay a hand on his slender body, and a snarling plunge for the offender's throat was Wolf's invariable reply to the caress.

It had been so since his puppyhood. He did not fly at accredited guests, nor, indeed, pay any heed to their presence, so long as they kept their hands off him. But to all of these the Boy was forced to say at the very outset of the visit:

"Pat Lad and Bruce all you want to, but please leave Wolf alone. He doesn't care for people. We've taught him to stand for a pat on the head, from guests,—but don't touch his body."

Then, to prove his own immunity, the Boy would proceed to tumble Wolf about, to the delight of them both.

In romping with humans whom they love, most dogs will bite, more or less gently,—or pretend to bite,—as a part of the game. Wolf never did this. In his wildest and roughest romps with the Boy or with the Boy's parents, Wolf did not so much as open his mighty jaws. Perhaps because he dared not trust himself to bite gently. Perhaps because he realised that a bite is not a joke, but an effort to kill.

There had been only one exception to Wolf's hatred for mauling at strangers' hands. A man came to The Place on a business call, bringing along a chubby two-year-old daughter. The Master warned the baby that she must not go near Wolf, although she

115

might pet any of the other collies. Then he became so much interested in the business talk that he and his guest forgot all about the child.

Ten minutes later the Master chanced to shift his gaze to the far end of the room. And he broke off, with a gasp, in the very middle of a sentence.

The baby was seated astride Wolf's back, her tiny heels digging into the dog's sensitive ribs, and each of her chubby fists gripping one of his ears. Wolf was lying there, with an idiotically happy grin on his face and wagging his tail in ecstasy.

No one knew why he had submitted to the baby's tugging hands, except because she was a baby, and because the gallant heart of the dog had gone out to her helplessness.

Wolf was the official watch-dog of The Place; and his name carried dread to the loafers and tramps of the region. Also, he was the Boy's own special dog. He had been born on the Boy's tenth birthday, five years before this story of ours begins; and ever since then the two had been inseparable chums.

One sloppy afternoon in late winter, Wolf and the Boy were sprawled, side by side; on the fur rug in front of the library fire. The Mistress and the Master had gone to town for the day. The house was lonely, and the two chums were left to entertain each other.

The Boy was reading a magazine. The dog beside him was blinking in drowsy comfort at the fire. Presently, finishing the story he had been reading, the Boy looked across at the sleepy dog.

"Wolf," he said, "here's a story about a dog. I think he must have been something like you. Maybe he was your great-great-great-great-grandfather. He lived an awfully long time ago—in Pompeii. Ever hear of Pompeii?"

Now, the Boy was fifteen years old, and he had too much sense to imagine that Wolf could possibly understand the story he was about to tell him. But, long since, he had fallen into a way of talking to his dog, sometimes, as if to another human. It was fun for him to note the almost pathetic eagerness wherewith Wolf listened and tried to grasp the meaning of what he was saying. Again and again, at sound of some familiar word or voice inflection, the collie would pick up his ears or wag his tail, as if in the joyous hope that he had at last found a clue to his owner's meaning.

"You see," went on the Boy, "this dog lived in Pompeii, as I told you. You've never been there, Wolf."

Wolf was looking up at the Boy in wistful excitement, seeking vainly to guess what was expected of him.

"And," continued the Boy, "the kid who owned him seems to

116

have had a regular knack for getting into trouble all the time. And his dog was always on hand to get him out of it. It's a true story, the magazine says. The kid's father was so grateful to the dog that he bought him a solid silver coller. Solid silver! Get that, Wolfie?"

Wolf did not "get it." But he wagged his tail hopefully, his eyes alight with bewildered interest.

"And," said the Boy, "what do you suppose was engraved on the collar? Well, I'll tell you: 'This dog has thrice saved his little master from death. Once by fire, once by flood, and once at the hands of robbers!' How's that for a record, Wolf? For one dog, too!"

At the words "Wolf" and "dog," the collie's tail smote the floor in glad comprehension. Then he edged closer to the Boy as the narrator's voice presently took on a sadder note.

"But at last," resumed the Boy, "there came a time when the dog couldn't save the kid. Mount Vesuvius erupted. All the sky was pitch-dark, as black as midnight, and Pompeii was buried under lava and ashes. The dog could easily have got away by himself,—dogs can see in the dark, can't they, Wolf?—but he couldn't get the kid away. And he wouldn't go without him. You wouldn't have gone without me, either, would you, Wolf? Pretty nearly two thousand years later, some people dug through the lava that covered Pompeii. What do you suppose they found? Of course they found a whole lot of things. One of them was that dog—silver collar and inscription and all. He was lying at the feet of a child. The child he couldn't save. He was one grand dog—hey, Wolf?"

The continued strain of trying to understand began to get on the collie's high-strung nerves. He rose to his feet, quivering, and sought to lick the Boy's face, thrusting one upraised white forepaw at him in appeal for a handshake. The Boy slammed shut the magazine.

"It's slow in the house, here, with nothing to do," he said to his chum. "I'm going up the lake with my gun to see if any wild ducks have landed in the marshes yet. It's almost time for them. Want to come along?"

The last sentence Wolf understood perfectly. On the instant he was dancing with excitement at the prospect of a walk. Being a collie, he was of no earthly help in a hunting-trip; but, on such tramps, as everywhere else, he was the Boy's inseparable companion.

Out over the slushy snow the two started, the Boy with his light single-barrelled shotgun slung over one shoulder, the dog trotting close at his heels. The March thaw was changing to a sharp freeze. The deep and soggy snow was crusted over, just thick enough to make walking a genuine difficulty for both dog and Boy.

117

The Place was a promontory that ran out into the lake, on the opposite bank from the mile-distant village. Behind, across the highroad, lay the winter-choked forest. At the lake's northerly end, two miles beyond The Place, were the reedy marshes where, a month hence, wild duck would congregate. Thither, with Wolf, the Boy ploughed his way through the biting cold.

The going was heavy and heavier. A quarter-mile below the marshes the Boy struck out across the upper corner of the lake. Here the ice was rotten at the top, where the thaw had nibbled at it, but beneath it was still a full eight inches thick; easily strong enough to bear the Boy's weight.

Along the grey ice-field the two plodded. The skim of water, which the thaw had spread an inch thick over the ice, had frozen in the day's cold spell. It crackled like broken glass as the chums walked over it. The Boy had on big hunting-boots. So, apart from the extra effort, the glass-like ice did not bother him. To Wolf it gave acute pain. The sharp particles were forever getting between the callous black pads of his feet, pricking and cutting him acutely.

Little smears of blood began to mark the dog's course but it never occurred to Wolf to turn back, or to betray by any sign that he was suffering. It was all a part of the day's work—a cheap price to pay for the joy of tramping with his adored young master.

Then, forty yards or so on the hither side of the marshes, Wolf beheld a right amazing phenomenon. The Boy had been walking directly in front of him, gun over shoulder. With no warning at all, the youthful hunter fell, feet foremost, out of sight, through the ice.

The light shell of new-frozen water that covered the lake's thicker ice also masked an air-hole nearly three feet wide. Into this, as he strode carelessly along, the Boy had stepped. Straight down he had gone, with all the force of his hundred-and-twenty pounds and with all the impetus of his forward stride.

Instinctively, he threw out his hands to restore his balance. The only effect of this was to send the gun flying ten feet away.

Down went the Boy through less than three feet of water (for the bottom of the lake at this point had started to slope upward towards the marshes) and through nearly two feet more of sticky marsh mud that underlay the lake-bed.

His outflung hands struck against the ice on the edges of the air-hole, and clung there.

Sputtering and gurgling, the Boy brought his head above the surface and tried to raise himself by his hands, high enough to wriggle out upon the surface of the ice. Ordinarily, this would have been simple enough for so strong a lad. But the glue-like mud had

118

imprisoned his feet and the lower part of his legs; and held them powerless.

Try as he would, the Boy could not wrench himself free of the slough. The water, as he stood upright, was on a level with his mouth. The air-hole was too wide for him, at such a depth, to get a good purchase on its edges and lift himself bodily to safety.

Gaining such a finger-hold as he could, he heaved with all his might, throwing every muscle of his body into the struggle. One leg was pulled almost free of the mud, but the other was driven deeper into it. And, as the Boy's fingers slipped from the smoothly wet ice-edge, the attempt to restore his balance drove the free leg back, knee-deep into the mire.

Ten minutes of this hopeless fighting left the Boy panting and tired out. The icy water was numbing his nerves and chilling his blood into torpidity. His hands were without sense of feeling, as far up as the wrists. Even if he could have shaken free his legs from the mud, now, he had not strength enough left to crawl out of the hole.

He ceased his useless frantic battle and stood dazed. Then he came sharply to himself. For, as he stood, the water crept upward from his lips to his nostrils. He knew why the water seemed to be rising. It was not rising. It was he who was sinking. As soon as he stopped moving, the mud began, very slowly, but very steadily, to suck him downward.

This was not a quicksand, but it was a deep mud-bed. And only by constant motion could he avoid sinking farther and farther down into it. He had less than two inches to spare, at best, before the water should fill his nostrils; less than two inches of life, even if he could keep the water down to the level of his lips.

There was a moment of utter panic. Then the Boy's brain cleared. His only hope was to keep on fighting—to rest when he must, for a moment or so, and then to renew his numbed grip on the ice-edge and try to pull his feet a few inches higher out of the mud. He must do this as long as his chilled body could be scourged into obeying his will.

He struggled again, but with virtually no result in raising himself. A second struggle, however, brought him chin-high above the water. He remembered confusedly that some of these earlier struggles had scarce budged him, while others had gained him two or three inches. Vaguely, he wondered why. Then turning his head, he realised.

Wolf, as he turned, was just loosing his hold on the wide collar of the Boy's mackinaw. His cut forepaws were still braced against a flaw of ragged ice on the air-hole's edge, and all his tawny body was tense.

His body was dripping wet, too. The Boy noted that; and he realised that the repeated effort to draw his master to safety must have resulted, at least once, in pulling the dog down into the water with the floundering Boy.

"Once more, Wolfie! Once more!" chattered the Boy through teeth that clicked together like castanets.

The dog darted forward, caught his grip afresh on the edge of the Boy's collar, and tugged with all his fierce strength; growling and whining ferociously the while.

The Boy seconded the collie's tuggings by a supreme struggle that lifted him higher than before. He was able to get one arm and shoulder clear. His numb fingers closed about an up-thrust tree-limb which had been washed down stream in the autumn freshets and had been frozen into the lake ice.

With this new purchase, and aided by the dog, the Boy tried to drag himself out of the hole. But the chill of the water had done its work. He had not the strength to move farther. The mud still sucked at his calves and ankles. The big hunting-boots were full of water that seemed to weigh a ton.

He lay there, gasping and chattering. Then through the gathering twilight, his eyes fell on the gun, lying ten feet away.

"Wolf!" he ordered, nodding towards the weapon. "Get it! Get it!"

Not in vain had the Boy talked to Wolf, for years, as if the dog were human. At the words and the nod, the collie trotted over to the gun, lifted it by the stock, and hauled it awkwardly along over the bumpy ice to his master, where he laid it down at the edge of the air-hole.

The dog's eyes were cloudy with trouble, and he shivered and whined as with ague. The water on his thick coat was freezing to a mass of ice. But it was from anxiety that he shivered, and not from cold.

Still keeping his numb grasp on the tree-branch, the boy balanced himself as best he could, and thrust two fingers of his free hand into his mouth to warm them into sensation again.

When this was done, he reached out to where the gun lay, and pulled its trigger. The shot boomed deafeningly through the twilight winter silences. The recoil sent the weapon sliding sharply back along the ice, spraining the Boy's trigger finger and cutting it to the bone.

"That's all I can do," said the Boy to himself. "If any one hears it, well and good. I can't get at another cartridge. I couldn't put it into the breech if I had it. My hands are too numb."

For several endless minutes he clung there, listening. But this was a desolate part of the lake, far from any road; and the season was too early for other hunters to be abroad. The bitter cold, in any case, tended to make sane folk hug the fireside rather than to venture so far into the open. Nor was the single report of a gun uncommon enough to call for investigation in such weather.

All this the Boy told himself, as the minutes dragged by. Then he looked again at Wolf. The dog, head on one side, still stood protectingly above him. The dog was cold and in pain. But, being only a dog, it did not occur to him to trot off home to the comfort of the library fire and leave his master to fend for himself.

Presently, with a little sigh, Wolf lay down on the ice, his nose across the Boy's arm. Even if he lacked strength to save his beloved master, he could stay and share the Boy's sufferings.

But the Boy himself thought otherwise. He was not at all minded to freeze to death, nor was he willing to let Wolf imitate the dog of Pompeii by dying helplessly at his master's side. Controlling for an instant the chattering of his teeth, he called:

"Wolf!"

The dog was on his feet again at the word; alert, eager.

"Wolf!" repeated the boy. "Go! Hear me? Go!"

He pointed homeward.

Wolf stared at him, hesitant. Again the Boy called in vehement command, "Go!"

The collie lifted his head to the twilight sky with a wolf-howl hideous in its grief and appeal—a howl as wild and discordant as that of any of his savage ancestors. Then, stooping first to lick the numb hand that clung to the branch, Wolf turned and fled.

Across the cruelly sharp film of ice he tore, at top speed, head down; whirling through the deepening dusk like a flash of tawny light.

Wolf understood what was wanted of him. Wolf always understood. The pain in his feet was as nothing. The stiffness of his numbed body was forgotten in the urgency for speed.

The Boy looked drearily after the swift-vanishing figure which the dusk was swallowing. He knew the dog would try to bring help; as has many another and lesser dog in times of need. Whether or not that help could arrive in time, or at all, was a point on which the Boy would not let himself dwell. Into his benumbed brain crept the memory of an old Norse proverb he had read in school:

"Heroism consists in hanging on, one minute longer."

Unconsciously he tightened his feeble hold on the tree-branch and braced himself.

121

From the marshes to The Place was a full two miles. Despite the deep and sticky snow, Wolf covered the distance in less than nine minutes. He paused in front of the gate-lodge, at the highway entrance to the drive. But the superintendent and his wife had gone to Paterson, shopping, that afternoon.

Down the drive to the house he dashed. The maids had taken advantage of their employers' day in New York, to walk across the lake to the village, to a motion-picture show.

Wise men claim that dogs have not the power to think or to reason things out in a logical way. So perhaps it was mere chance that next sent Wolf's flying feet across the lake to the village. Perhaps it was chance, and not the knowledge that where there is a village there are people.

Again and again, in the car, he had sat upon the front seat alongside the Mistress when she drove to the station to meet guests. There were always people at the station. And to the station Wolf now raced.

The usual group of platform idlers had been dispersed by the cold. A solitary baggageman was hauling a trunk and some boxes out of the express-coop on to the platform; to be put aboard the five o'clock train from New York.

As the baggageman passed under the clump of station lights, he came to a sudden halt. For out of the darkness dashed a dog. Full tilt, the animal rushed up to him and seized him by the skirt of the overcoat.

The man cried out in scared surprise. He dropped the box he was carrying and struck at the dog, to ward off the seemingly murderous attack. He recognised Wolf, and he knew the collie's repute.

But Wolf was not attacking. Holding tight to the coat-skirt, he backed away, trying to draw the man with him, and all the while whimpering aloud like a nervous puppy.

A kick from the heavy-shod boot broke the dog's hold on the coat-skirt, even as a second yell from the man brought four or five other people running out from the station waiting-room.

One of these, the telegraph operator, took in the scene at a single glance. With great presence of mind he bawled loudly:

"Mad dog!"

This, as Wolf, reeling from the kick, sought to gain another grip on the coat-skirt. A second kick sent him rolling over and over on the tracks, while other voices took up the panic cry of "Mad dog!"

Now, a mad dog is supposed to be a dog afflicted by rabies. Once in ten thousand times, at the very most, a mad-dog hue-and-

122

cry is justified. Certainly not oftener. A harmless and friendly dog loses his master on the street. He runs about, confused and frightened, looking for the owner he has lost. A boy throws a stone at him. Other boys chase him. His tongue hangs out, and his eyes glaze with terror. Then some fool bellows:

"Mad dog!"

And the cruel chase is on—a chase that ends in the pitiful victim's death. Yes, in every crowd there is a voice ready to raise that asinine and murderously cruel shout.

So it was with the men who witnessed Wolf's frenzied effort to take aid to the imperilled Boy.

Voice after voice repeated the cry. Men groped along the platform edge for stones to throw. The village policeman ran puffingly upon the scene, drawing his revolver.

Finding it useless to make a further attempt to drag the baggageman to the rescue, Wolf leaped back, facing the ever larger group. Back went his head again in that hideous wolf-howl. Then he galloped away a few yards, trotted back, howled once more, and again galloped lakeward.

All of which only confirmed the panicky crowd in the belief that they were threatened by a mad dog. A shower of stones hurtled about Wolf as he came back a third time to lure these dull humans into following him.

One pointed rock smote the collie's shoulder, glancingly, cutting it to the bone. A shot from the policeman's revolver fanned the fur of his ruff, as it whizzed past.

Knowing that he faced death, he nevertheless stood his ground, not troubling to dodge the fusillade of stones, but continuing to run lakeward and then trot back, whining with excitement.

A second pistol-shot flew wide. A third grazed the dog's hip. From all directions people were running towards the station. A man darted into a house next door, and emerged carrying a shot-gun. This he steadied on the veranda-rail not forty feet away from the leaping dog, and made ready to fire.

It was then the train from New York came in. And, momentarily, the sport of "mad-dog" killing was abandoned, while the crowd scattered to each side of the track.

From a front car of the train the Mistress and the Master emerged into a bedlam of noise and confusion.

"Best hide in the station, Ma'am!" shouted the telegraph operator, at sight of the Mistress. "There is a mad dog loose out here! He's chasing folks around, and—"

"Mad dog!" repeated the Mistress in high contempt. "If you knew anything about dogs, you'd know mad ones never 'chase folks around,' any more than diphtheria patients do. Then—"

A flash of tawny light beneath the station lamp, a scurrying of frightened idlers, a final wasted shot from the policeman's pistol,— as Wolf dived headlong through the frightened crowd towards the voice he heard and recognised.

Up to the Mistress and the Master galloped Wolf. He was bleeding, his eyes were bloodshot, his fur was rumpled. He seized the astounded Master's gloved hand lightly between his teeth and sought to pull him across the tracks and towards the lake.

The Master knew dogs. Especially he knew Wolf. And without a word he suffered himself to be led. The Mistress and one or two inquisitive men followed.

Presently, Wolf loosed his hold on the Master's hand and ran on ahead, darting back every few moments to make certain he was followed.

"Heroism—consists—in—hanging—on—one—minute— longer," the Boy was whispering deliriously to himself for the hundredth time; as Wolf pattered up to him in triumph, across the ice, with the human rescuers a scant ten yards behind.

EIGHT

Afterword

I have drawn upon one of our Sunnybank collies for the name and the aspect and certain traits of my "Treve" book's hero. The real Treve was my chum, and one of the strangest and most beautiful collies I have known.

Dog aristocrats have two names; one whereby they are registered in the American Kennel Club's immortal studbook and one by which they are known at home. The first of these is called the "pedigree name." The second is the "kennel name." Few dogs know or answer to their own high-sounding pedigree names. In speaking to them their kennel names alone are used.

For example, my grand old Bruce's pedigree name was Sunnybank Goldsmith;—a term that meant nothing to him. My Champion Sunnybank Sigurdson (greatest of Treve's sons), responds only to the name of "Squire." Sunnybank Lochinvar is "Roy."

Treve's pedigree name was "Sunnybank Sigurd." And in time he won his right to the hard-sought and harder-earned prefix of "CHAMPION";—the supreme crown of dogdom.

We named him Sigurd—the Mistress and I—in honour of the collie of Katharine Lee Bates; a dog made famous the world over by his owner's exquisite book, "Sigurd, Our Golden Collie."

But here difficulties set in.

It is all very well to shout "Sigurd!" to a collie when he is the only dog in sight. But when there is a rackety and swirling and excited throng of them, the call of "Sigurd!" has an unlucky sibilant resemblance to the exhortation, "Sic 'im!" And misunderstandings— not to say strife—are prone to follow. So we sought a one-syllable kennel name for our golden collie pup. My English superintendent, Robert Friend, suggested "Treve."

The pup took to it at once.

He was red-gold-and-snow of coat; a big slender youngster, with the true "look of eagles" in his deepset dark eyes. In those eyes, too, burned an eternal imp of mischief.

I have bred or otherwise acquired hundreds of collies in my time. No two of them were alike. That is the joy of collies. But most of them had certain well-defined collie characteristics in common with their blood-brethren. Treve had practically none. He was not like other collies or like a dog of any breed.

Gloriously beautiful, madly alive in every inch of him, he combined the widest and most irreconcilable range of traits.

For him there were but three people on earth;—the Mistress, myself and Robert Friend. To us he gave complete allegiance, if in queer form. The rest of mankind, with one exception—a girl—did not exist, so far as he was concerned; unless the rest of mankind undertook to speak to him or to pat him. Then, instantly, such familiarity was rewarded by a murderous growl and a most terrifying bite.

The bite was delivered with a frightful show of ferocity. And it had not the force to crush the wing of a fly.

Strangers, assailed thus, were startled. Some were frankly scared. They would stare down in amaze at the bitten surface, marvelling that there was neither blood nor teeth-mark nor pain. For the attack always had an appearance of man-eating fury.

Treve would allow the Mistress to pat him—in moderation. But if I touched him, in friendliness, he would toss his beautiful head and dart out of reach, barking angrily back at me. It was the same when Robert tried to pet him.

Once or twice a day he would come up to me, laying his head across my arm or knee; growling with the utmost vehemence and gnawing at my sleeve for a minute at a time. I gather that this was a form of affection. He did it to nobody else.

Also, when I went to town for the day, he would mope around for awhile; then would take my cap from the hall table and carry it into my study. All day long he would lie there, one paw on the cap, and growl fierce menace to all who ventured near. On my return home at night, he gave me scarcely a glance and drew disgustedly away as usual when I held out my hand to pat him.

In the evenings, on the porch or in front of the living room fire, he would stroll unconcernedly about until he made sure I was not noticing. Then he would curl himself on the floor in front of me, pressing his furry body close to my ankles; and would lie there for hours.

The Mistress alone he forbore to bite. He loved her. But she was a grievous disappointment to him. From the first, she saw through his vehement show of ferocity and took it at its true value. Try as he would he could not frighten her. Try as he would, he could not mask his adoration for her.

Again and again he would lie down for a nap at her feet; only to waken presently with a thundrous growl and a snarl, and with a lunge of bared teeth at her caressing hand. The hand would continue to caress; and his show of fury was met with a laugh and with the comment:

"You've had a good sleep, and now you've waked up in a nice homicidal rage."

Failing to alarm her, the dog would look sheepishly at the laughing face and then cuddle down again at her feet to be petted.

There was another side to his play of indifference and of wrath. True, he would toss his head and back away, barking, when Robert or myself tried to pat him. But at the quietly spoken word, "Treve!", he would come straight up to us and, if need be, stand statue-like for an hour at a time, while he was groomed or otherwise handled.

In brief, he was the naughtiest and at the same time the most unfailingly obedient dog I have owned. No matter how far away he might be, the single voicing of his name would bring him to me in a swirling rush.

In the show-ring he was a problem. At times he showed as proudly and as spectacularly as any attitude-striking tragedian. Again, if he did not chance to like his surroundings or if the ring-side crowd displeased him, he prepared to loaf in slovenly fashion through his paces on the block and in the parade. At such times the showing of Treve became as much an art as is the guiding of a temperamental race-horse to victory. It called for tact; even for trickery.

In the first place, during these fits of ill-humour, he would start around the ring, in the preliminary parade, with his tail arched high over his back; although he knew, as well as did I, that a collie's tail should be carried low, in the ring.

I commanded: "Tail down!" Down would come the tail. But at the same time would come a savage growl and a sensational snap at my wrist. The spectators pointed out to one another the incurably fierce collie. Fellow-exhibitors in the ring would edge away. The judge—if he were an outsider—would eye Treve with strong apprehension.

It was the same when I whispered, "Foot out!" as he deliberately turned one white front toe inward in coming to a halt on the judging block. A similar snarl and feather-light snap followed the command.

The worst part of the ordeal came when the judge began to "go over" him with expert hands, to test the levelness of his mouth, the spring of his ribs, his general soundness and the texture of his coat. An exhibitor is not supposed to speak to a judge in the ring

127

except to answer a question. But if the judge were inspecting Treve for the first time, I used to mumble conciliatingly, the while:

"He's only in play, Judge. The dog's perfectly gentle."

This, as Treve resented the stranger's handling, by growl-fringed bites at the nearest part of the judicial anatomy.

A savage dog does not make a hit with the average judge. There is scant joyance in being chewed, in the pursuit of one's judging-duties. Yet, as a rule, judges took my word as to Treve's gentleness; especially after one sample of his biteless biting. Said Vinton Breese, the famed "all-rounder" dog-judge, after an Interstate show:

"I feel slighted. Sigurd forgot to bite me to-day. It's the first time."

The Mistress made up a little song, in which Treve's name occurred oftener than almost all its other words. Treve was inordinately proud of this song. He would stand, growling softly, with his head on his side, for an indefinite time, listening to her sing it. He used to lure her into chanting this super-personal ditty by trotting to the piano and then running back to her.

Nature intended him for a staunch, clever, implicitly obedient, gentle collie, without a single bad trait, and possessed of rare sweetness. He tried his best to make himself thoroughly mean and savage and treacherous. He met with pitifully poor success in his chosen rôle. The sweetness and the obedient gentleness stuck forth, past all his best efforts to mask them in ferocity.

Once, when he bit with overmuch unction at a guest who tried to pat him, I spoke sharply to him and emphasised my rebuke by a slight slap on the shoulder. The dog was heart-broken. Crouching at my feet, his head on my boot, he sobbed exactly like a frightened child. He spent hours trying pitifully to make friends with me again.

It was so when his snarl and his nip at the legs of one of the other dogs led to warlike retaliation. At once Treve would rush to me for protection and for comfort. From the safe haven of my knees he would hurl threats at his assailant and defy him to carry the quarrel further. There was no fight in him. At the same time there was no taint of cowardice. He bore pain or discomfort or real danger unflinchingly.

One of his chief joys was to ransack the garage and stables for sponges and rags which were stored there for cleaning the cars. These he would carry, one by one, to the long grass or to the lake, and deposit them there. When the men hid these choice playthings out of his way he would stand on his hindlegs and explore the shelves and low beam-corners in search of them; never resting till he found one or more to bear off.

He would lug away porch cushions and carelessly-deserted hats and wraps, and deposit them in all sorts of impossible places; never by any chance bringing them back.

From puppyhood, he did not once eat a whole meal of his own accord. Always he must be fed by hand. Even then he would not touch any food but cooked meat.

Normally, the solution to this would have been to let him go hungry until he was ready to eat. But a valuable show-and-stud collie cannot be allowed to become a skeleton and lifeless for lack of food, any more than a winning race-horse can be permitted to starve away his strength and speed.

Treve's daily pound-and-a-half of broiled chuck steak was cut in small pieces and set before him on a plate. Then began the eternal task of making him eat it. Did we turn our backs on him for a single minute—the food had vanished when next we looked.

But it had not vanished down Treve's dainty throat. Casual search revealed every missing morsel of meat shoved neatly out of sight under the edges of the plate or else hidden in the grass or under nearby boards or handfuls of straw.

This daily meal was a game. Treve enjoyed it immensely. Not being blessed with patience, I abhorred it. So Robert Friend took the duty of feeding him. At sound of Robert's distant knife, whetted to cut up the meat, Treve would come flying to the hammock where I sat writing. At a bound he was in my lap, all fours and all fur—the entire sixty pounds of him—and with his head thrust under one of the hammock cushions.

Thence, at Robert's call, and at my own exhortation, he would come forth with mincing reluctance and approach the tempting dish of broiled steak. Looking coldly upon the food, he would lie down. To all of Robert's allurements to eat, the dog turned a deaf ear. Once in a blue moon, he consented to swallow the steak, piece by piece, if Robert would feed it to him by hand. Oftener it was necessary to call on Wolf to act as stimulant to appetite.

"Then I'll give it to Wolf," Robert would threaten. "Wolf!"

Treve got to his feet with head lowered and teeth bared. Robert called Wolf, who came lazily to play his part in the daily game for a guerdon of one piece of the meat.

Six feet away from the dish, Wolf paused. But his work was done. Growling, barking, roaring, Treve attacked the dish; snatching up and bolting one morsel of meat at a time. Between every two bites he bellowed threats and insults at the placidly watching Wolf,—Wolf who could thrash his weight in tigers and who, after Lad and Bruce died, was the acknowledged king of all the Place's dogs.

In this way, mouthful by mouthful and with an accompaniment of raging noise that could be heard across the lake, Treve disposed of his dinner.

Yes, it was a silly thing to humour him in the game. But there was no other method of making him eat the food on which depended his continued show-form and his dynamite vitality. When it came to giving him his two raw eggs a day, there was nothing to that but forcible feeding. In solid cash prizes and in fees, Treve paid back, by many hundred per cent., the high cost of his food.

When he was little more than a puppy, he fell dangerously ill with some kind of heart trouble. Dr. Hopper said he must have medicine every half hour, day and night, until he should be better. I sat up with him for two nights.

I got little enough work done, between times, on those two nights. The suffering dog, lay on a rug beside my study desk. But he was uneasy and wanted to be talked to. He was in too much pain to go to sleep. In a corner of my study was a tin biscuit box, which I kept filled with animal crackers, as occasional titbits for the collies. Every now and then, during our two-night vigil, I took an animal cracker from the box and fed it to Treve.

By the second night he was having a beautiful time. I was not.

The study seemed to him a most delightful place. Forthwith he adopted it as his lair. By the third morning he was out of danger and indeed was practically well again. But he had acquired the study-habit; a habit which lasted throughout his short life.

From that time on, it was Treve's study; not mine. The tin cracker box became his treasure chest; a thing to be guarded as jealously as ever was the Nibelungen Hoard or the Koh-i-noor.

If he chanced to be lying in any other room, and a dog unconsciously walked between him and the study, Treve bounded up from the soundest sleep and rushed growlingly to the study door, whence he snarled defiance at the possible intruder. If he were in the study and another dog ventured near, Treve's teeth were bared and Treve's fore-feet were planted firmly atop the tin box; as he ordered away the potential despoiler of his hoard.

No human, save only the Mistress and myself, might enter the study unchallenged. Grudgingly, Treve conceded her right and mine to be there. But a rush at the ankles of any one else discouraged ingress. I remember my daughter stopped in there one day to speak to me; on her way for a swim. As the bathing-dressed figure appeared on the threshold, Treve made a snarling rush for it. Alternately and vehemently he bit both bare ankles.

"I wish he wouldn't do that," complained my daughter, annoyed. "He tickles so when he bites!"

No expert trainer has worked more skilfully and tirelessly over a Derby winner than did Robert Friend over that dog's shimmering red-gold coat. For an hour or more every day, he groomed Treve, until the burnished fur stood out like a Circassian beauty's coiffure and glowed like molten gold. The dog stood moveless throughout the long and tedious process; except when he obeyed the order to turn to one side or the other or to lift his head or to put up his paws for a brushing of the silken sleeve-ruffles.

It was Robert, too, who hit on the scheme which gave Treve his last show-victory; when the collie already had won fourteen of the needful fifteen points which should make him a Champion of Record.

Perhaps you think it is easy to pilot even the best of dogs through the gruelling ordeals that go to make up those fifteen points. Well, it is not.

Many breeders take their dogs on the various show-circuits, keeping them on the bench for three days at a time; and then, week after week, shipping them in stuffy crates from town to town, from show to show. In this way, the championship points sometimes pile up with reasonable speed;—and sometimes never at all. (Sometimes, too, the luckless dog is found dead in his crate, on arriving at the show-hall. Oftener he catches distemper and dies in more painful and leisurely fashion.)

I am too foolishly mush-hearted to inflict such torture on any of our Sunnybank collies. I never take my dogs to a show that cannot be reached by comfortable motor ride within two or three hours at most; nor to any show whence they cannot return home at the end of a single day. Thus, championship points mount up more slowly at Sunnybank than at some other kennels. But thus, too, our dogs, for the most part, stay alive and in splendid health. I sleep the sounder at night, for knowing my collie chums are not in misery in some distemper-tainted dogshow-building.

In like manner, it is a fixed rule with us never to ship a Sunnybank puppy anywhere by express to a purchaser People must come here in person and take home the pups they buy from me. Buyers have motored to Sunnybank for pups from Maine and Ohio and even from California.

These scruples of mine have earned me the good-natured guying of more sensible collie breeders.

Well, Treve had picked up fourteen of the fifteen points needed to complete his championship. The last worthwhile show of the spring season—within motor distance—was at Noble, Pa., on June 10, 1922. Incidentally, June 10, 1922, was Treve's third birthday. His wonderful coat was at the climax of its shining fulness. By autumn he would be "out of coat"; and an out-of-coat collie stands small chance of winning.

So Robert and I drove over to Noble with him.

The day was stewingly hot; the drive was long. Show-goers crowded around the splendid dog before the judging began. Bit by bit, Treve's nerves began to fray. We kept him off his bench and in the shade, and we did what we could to steer admirers away from him. But it was no use. By the time the collie division was called into the tented ring, Treve was profoundly unhappy and cranky.

He slouched in, with no more "form" to him than a plough horse. With the rest of his class ("Open, sable-and-white"), he went through the parade. Judge Cooper called the contestants one by one up to the block; Treve last of all. My best efforts could not rouse the dog from his sullen apathy.

It was then that Robert Friend played his trump card. Standing just outside the ring, among the jam of spectators, he called excitedly:

"Wolf! I'll give it to Wolf!"

I don't know what the other spectators thought of this outburst. But I know the effect it had on Treve.

In a flash the great dog was alert and tense; his tulip ears up, his whole body at attention, the look of eagles in his eyes as he scanned the ringside for a glimpse of his friend, Wolf.

Judge Cooper took one long look at him. Then, without so much as laying a hand on the magnificently-showing Treve, he awarded him the blue ribbon in his class.

I had sense enough to take the dog into one corner and to keep him there, quieting and steadying him until the Winners' Class was called. As I led him into the ring, then, to compete with the other classes' blue ribboners, Robert called once more to the absent Wolf. Again the trick served. The collie moved and stood as if galvanised into sparkling life.

Cooper handed me the Winners' rosette; the rosette whose acquisition made Treve a Champion of Record!

It was only about a year ago. In that little handful of time, the judge who made him a champion—the new-made champion himself—the dog whose name roused him from his apathy in the ring—all three are dead. I don't think a white sportsman like Cooper would mind my linking his name with two such supreme collies, in this word of necrology. Cooper—Treve—Wolf!

(There's lots of room in this old earth of ours for the digging of graves, isn't there?)

Home we came with our champion—Champion Sunnybank Sigurd—who displayed so little championship dignity that, an hour after our return to the Place, he lifted my brand new Panama hat daintily from the hall-table, carried it forth from the house with a loving tenderness; laid it to rest in a patch of lakeside mud; and then rolled on it.

I was too elated over our triumph to scold him for the costly sacrilege. I am glad now that I didn't. For a scolding or a single harsh word ever reduced him to utter heartbreak.

And so for a while, at the Place, our golden champion continued to revel in the gay zest of life.

He was the livest dog I have known. Wolf alone was his chum among all the Sunnybank collies. Wolf alone, with his mighty heart and vast wisdom and his elfin sense of fun and his love for frolic. Wolf and Treve used to play a complicated game whose chief move consisted of a sweeping breakneck gallop, for perhaps a half-mile, to the accompaniment of a fanfare of barking. Across the green lawns they would flash, like red-gold meteors; and at a pace none of their fleet-footed brethren could maintain.

One morning they started as usual on this whirlwind dash. But at the end of the first few yards, Treve swayed in his flying stride, faltered to a stop and came slowly back to me. He thrust his muzzle into my cupped hand—for the first time in his undemonstrative life—then stood wearily beside me.

A strange transformation had come over him. The best way I can describe it is to say that the glowing inward fire which always had seemed to shine through him—even to the flaming bright mass of coat—was gone. He was all at once old and sedate and massive; a dog of elderly dignity—a dignity oddly majestic. The mischief imp had fled from his eyes; the sheen and sunlight had vanished from his coat. He had ceased to be Treve.

I sent in a rush for the nearest good vet. The doctor examined the invalid with all the skilled attention due a dog whose cash value runs into four figures. Then he gave verdict.

It was the heart;—the heart that had been flighty in puppyhood days, but which two competent vets had since pronounced as sound as the traditional bell.

For a day longer the collie lived;—at least a gravely gentle and majestic collie lived in the marvellous body that had been Treve's. He did not suffer—or so the doctor told us—and he was content to stay very close to me; his paw or his head on my foot.

At last, stretching himself drowsily to sleep, he died.

It seemed impossible that such a swirl of glad life and

mischief and beauty could have been wiped out in twenty-four little hours.

Not for our virtues nor for our general worthiness are we remembered wistfully by those who stay on. Not for our sterling qualities are we cruelly missed when missing is futile. Worthiness, in its death, does not leave behind it the grinding heartache that comes at memory of some lovably naughty or mischievous or delightfully perverse trait.

Treve's entertaining badnesses had woven themselves into the very life of the Place. Their passing left a keen hurt. The more so because, under them, lay bedrock of staunch loyalty and gentleness.

I have not the skill to paint our eccentrically lovable chum's word picture, except in this clumsily written sketch. If I were to attempt to make a whole book of him, the result would be a daub.

But I have tried at least to make his name remembered by a few readers; by giving it to the hero of the "Treve" collection of stories. Perhaps some one, reading, may like the name, even if not the stories, and may call his or her next collie, "Treve"; in memory of a gallant dog that was dear to Sunnybank.

We buried him in the woods, near the house, here. A granite boulder serves as his headstone.

Alongside that boulder, a few days ago, we buried the Mistress's hero collie, Wolf; close to his old-time playmate, Treve.

Perhaps you may care to hear a word or two of Wolf's plucky death. Some of you have read his adventures in my other dog stories. More of you read of his passing. For nearly every newspaper in America printed a long account of it.

It is an account worth reading and rereading; as is every tale of clean courage. I am going to quote part of the finely-written story that appeared in the New York Times of June 28, 1923; a story far beyond power of mine to improve on or to equal:

"Wolf, son of Lad, is dead. The shaggy collie, with the eyes that understood and the friendly tail, made famous in the stories of Albert Payson Terhune, died like a thoroughbred. So when Wolf joined his father, in the canine Beyond, last Sunday night, there was no hanging of heads.

"Wolf died a hero. But yesterday the level lawns of Sunnybank, the Terhune place at Pompton Lakes, N. J., seemed empty and the big house was curiously quiet. True, other collies were there; but so, too, was the big boulder out in the woods with just 'Wolf' graven across it.

"Ten years ago, when thousands of readers were following Lad's career as told by his owner, Mr. Terhune, an interesting event

134

took place at Sunnybank. Of all the puppies that had or have come to Sunnybank, that group of newcomers was the most mischievous. Admittedly, Lad was properly proud, but readers will remember his occasional misgivings about one of the pups. The cause of parental concern was Wolf. He was a good puppy, you know, but a trifle boisterous; maybe—yes, he was, the littlest bit inclined to wildness.

"In 1918 Lad passed on; and the whole country mourned his departure. Wolf succeeded his famous father in the stories of Mr. Terhune. The son had long since abandoned his harum-scarum ways and had developed into a model member of the Terhune dog circle. Wolf was the property and the pet of Mrs. Terhune.

"He became the cleverest of all the collies. One could talk to Wolf and get understanding and no back talk. One could depend on Wolf and get full loyalty. One could like Wolf and say so; and the soft cool nose would come poking around and the tail would begin to wag till it seemed as if Wolf would wag himself off his feet.

"Wolf constituted himself warden of the Sunnybank lawns and custodian of the driveways. When motoring parties came in and endangered the lives of the puppies playing about the driveways, Wolf, at the first sound of the motor, would dash importantly down into the drive and would herd or chase every puppy out of harm's way.

"Each evening it was the habit of Wolf to saunter off on a long 'walk.' Three evenings ago he rambled away and—

"Down in the darkness at the railroad station some folk were waiting to see the Stroudsburg express flash by. It was a few minutes late. A nondescript dog, with a hunted, homeless droop to his tail, trotted onto the tracks.

"Far down the line there came the warning screech of the express. The canine tramp didn't pay any attention to it, but sat down to scratch at a flea.

"The headlight of the express shot a beam glistening along the rails. Wolf saw the dog and the danger. With a bark and a snap, the son of Lad thrust the stranger off the track and drove him to safety.

"The express was whistling, for a crossing, far past the station, when they picked up what was Wolf and started for the Terhune home."

All dogs die too soon. Many humans don't die soon enough. A dog is only a dog. And a dog is too gorgeously normal, and wholesome to be made ridiculous in death by his owner's sloppy sentimentality.

The stories of one's dogs, like the recital of one's dreams, are of no special interest to others. Perhaps I have talked overlong

135

about these two collie chums of ours. Belatedly, I ask your forgiveness if I have bored you.

Albert Payson Terhune

"Sunnybank,"
Pompton Lakes,
New Jersey.

136